HOME BEFORE DARK

As her headlights raked through the trees next to the cleared area, she jammed on the brakes. His car nestled among the trees at the edge of the clearing.

Immobilized, Sara clutched the steering wheel, her hands slippery with sweat. She felt as if she couldn't breathe, and her heart was pounding so hard she thought her chest would explode. It's him, she thought wildly. And Julie must be there with him . . . Fear emanated from her like a bad smell.

Lions

More heart-stopping Nightmares . . .

NIGHTMARES

HOME BEFORE DARK

Beverly Hastings

Lions
An Imprint of HarperCollinsPublishers

First published in the USA in 1993 by Berkley Books
First published in Great Britain in Lions in 1994

1 3 5 7 9 10 8 6 4 2

Lions is an imprint of HarperCollins Children's Books,
a division of HarperCollins Publishers Ltd, 77-85 Fulham
Palace Road, Hammersmith, London W6 8JB

Text copyright © 1993 by Beverly Hastings

ISBN 0 00 675017 6

Printed and bound in Great Britain
by HarperCollins Manufacturing Ltd, Glasgow

*For Carmela, a dear friend
whose energy and enthusiasm
are an inspiration*

PROLOGUE

Late-afternoon sunlight filtered through the new-green leaves of maple trees lining the old country road. Through the open window of his car, the driver sniffed the soft spring air blowing in. He turned to smile at the girl on the passenger seat beside him.

Mary Jo smiled back at him. "It was nice of you to give me a ride," she said. "It's a long walk home."

The driver grinned and shrugged his shoulders. "Hey, what's the point of having a car if you can't use it to have a little fun?"

Mary Jo leaned back against the seat and closed her eyes, enjoying the feel of the warm sun on her face. Then the car bounced over a bump in the road and her eyes flew open. She glanced out the window.

"This isn't the way to my house," she said with a tremor of uncertainty in her voice.

"Yes, it is," he told her in a reassuring tone. "It's just the long way around. Couldn't resist taking a little detour, what with such a gorgeous day outside and such a pretty girl sitting here next to me." He saw her blush and figured that not many guys had called her pretty. He smiled at her. Already his heart was thumping a little faster in anticipation of what was coming next.

The car turned down a rutted lane, passing a rusted For Sale sign—FORTY ACRES OF PASTURE, WILL SUBDIVIDE. Nervously Mary Jo pushed at strands of straight brown hair blowing across her face and tucked them behind her ears. "Where are you going?" This time her tone was sharper.

He didn't answer. Then he pulled to a stop near the trunk of an ancient chestnut tree and killed the engine. "Come on, let's take a walk." He sensed her reluctance, the faint beginnings of her fear. Already she was sorry she'd accepted a ride with him. "Come on," he urged. "We'll just stop here a couple of minutes. I promise."

Walking around the car, he opened the passenger door and reached for her hand. The girl's fear was mounting but she didn't want to cause a fuss, so she let him help her out of the car and lead her along a path under the trees toward an old deserted barn.

Mary Jo dragged her feet and he knew that she wouldn't willingly go inside the building. Spotting a soft patch of new spring grass, he led her toward it and then said, "Here, let's sit down."

"I don't want to," she told him, her voice trembling. "It's getting late. I'm supposed to be home before dark."

Ignoring her protest, he grasped her wrist tightly and dropped to the ground, pulling her down beside him. He put his arm around her shoulders, drawing her close. Startled, she didn't react for a second; then she tried to push him away. But he was strong, much stronger than she'd thought. As he tried to kiss her she twisted her face away from his. "No, don't. Let go of me."

His arm still pinned her against his body. "Hey, relax, it's going to be fine, you're going to like it."

"No!" Her voice was louder this time, but he paid no attention. Instead he grabbed her chin with one hand and turned her face back toward him.

Mary Jo screamed and flailed at him with her fists, but he just laughed. Helpless tears spilled down her cheeks. "I'll tell my dad," she whimpered.

"No, you won't." His voice was low. He pushed her back on the ground and she felt his heavy forearm across her throat.

The sun was lower in the sky when he stirred and slowly rose to his feet. Mary Jo's body lay totally still on the patch of spring grass.

He stood there for a moment, looking down at her. Then, shaking his head, he went back to his car and opened the trunk. Pushing aside the assortment of tools, he pulled out an old blanket. Too bad, he thought as he wrapped the girl's body in the blanket and began to carry it back toward his car. Too bad it ended like this. But she had asked for it.

CHAPTER 1

Sara Langdon gazed out the airplane window at the neatly delineated patches of farmland and miniature towns. It had been a long time since she'd visited Aunt Liz and Uncle Ted, so long ago that her mom had still been alive and her dad had just been a junior professor at UCLA instead of head of a whole department like he was now. Her memory of that two-week summer vacation was hazy in her mind. Mostly it was of swimming in the local pool and climbing apple trees with the kids who lived down the block from Aunt Liz. Now Overton, Ohio, the town where Aunt Liz and Uncle Ted lived, felt like a foreign country to her. And she was going to be stuck here for a whole year.

Why hadn't Dad let her stay at her best friend Patti's house? Sara wondered for the millionth time. She and Patti were sure they could work it out with Patti's mom, but before they even got the chance, Sara's dad had made his pronouncement. "Honey, it'll be great to live in a totally different part of the country for a year!" he'd told her with enthusiasm. "Lots of kids would give anything to go off and live with another family, make new friends, see new sights. . . ." He'd trailed off at that point, seeing what he called Sara's "mule frown." But he didn't give up trying to tell her what a great trip it was going to be.

When Sara heard her dad on the phone with Aunt Liz, she could tell that his older sister was really looking forward to Sara's arrival. There was no getting out of it, she finally realized. Might as well try to make the best of it.

Aunt Liz and Uncle Ted were waiting at the gate when Sara got off the plane. "Oh, it's so good to see you!" Aunt Liz said as she threw her arms around Sara. "And you've really grown," she continued.

"Either that or you've shrunk," Sara said with a laugh. At five-foot-six she was almost three inches taller than her aunt.

Uncle Ted leaned down and gave Sara a big bear hug. "She's turned into quite a looker, hasn't she, Liz?" he said, releasing Sara and giving her a broad wink. "Let's go, girls, and get the luggage sorted out."

Throughout the drive back to Overton Aunt Liz kept up a stream of enthusiastic and welcoming chatter. She wanted to know all about how Sara's dad was doing and what in the world possessed him to take his sabbatical in Brazil to do research on birds in the upper reaches of the Amazon. "I mean, he must be nuts. Who could stand to be in a jungle for a whole year?" she asked. But no response was necessary since Aunt Liz went on to answer her own question. "Of course he was always like that—get his teeth into a project and the whole house could catch on fire before he'd even smell smoke."

As they unloaded the car Aunt Liz went on, "I hope you'll excuse the way your room looks. It's a total disaster. I wasn't sure about how to do up the guest room for you—I mean, with my clients I spend time getting to know what they like to do and stuff like that before I suggest color schemes and furniture and room arrangements. But we're going to have a great time picking stuff out, Sara. Oh, I'm so glad you're here!"

Of course the guest room was far from a disaster. In fact, the whole house looked like something out of a magazine. Sara didn't remember her aunt and uncle's house being so glamorous before; then she realized that Aunt Liz hadn't been in the decorating business the last time Sara had visited. Even before Uncle Ted had finished lugging all three of Sara's big suitcases up the stairs, Aunt Liz was pulling out fabric samples and sketches of possible ways to redesign the room that would be Sara's for the next year.

"For Pete's sake, Liz, let the girl catch her breath," Uncle Ted said as he plopped the last suitcase on the extra bed. He winked at Sara and then put his arm around his wife's shoulders. "Why don't you girls get ready and I'll take you to Oscar's for dinner."

Sara had just spent the entire day sitting in an airplane being fed nonstop while flying through three time zones. The clock on the nightstand said 6:23 P.M., but for Sara it was still the middle of the afternoon. The last thing she wanted to do was go to some fancy restaurant. But the look on Aunt Liz's face as she smiled up at her husband made Sara's protests die unsaid.

As it turned out, going out to dinner wasn't so bad. Oscar's was on a road outside of town, miles from anywhere as far as Sara could tell. The drive took them past acres of farmland with only the occasional farmhouse and barn to remind them of civilization, and by the time they'd turned onto a narrow unmarked road, Sara didn't know what to expect. But the restaurant, nestled in a grove of huge trees and overlooking a burbling brook, was full of rustic charm. The service and food were certainly as good as anything Sara had encountered in Los Angeles. In fact, she surprised herself by wolfing down a huge steak and dessert as well. Maybe it was all that clean, fresh country air.

Walking outside after they'd finished, Sara lagged behind her aunt and uncle. In the still, soft September air she could hear the chortle of the stream and the rustle of the trees overhead. She looked up and saw a skyful of stars, something she'd never seen in L.A. Maybe spending a year in Ohio wouldn't be so bad.

Uncle Ted held the door open for her and Sara climbed into the backseat of his dark blue Lincoln Town Car and nestled back against the buttery leather upholstery. "What did you think of Oscar's, Sara?" he asked her as he started the car.

"It was great," she replied truthfully.

"So I guess we're not just a bunch of small-town hicks, huh?" he asked. His tone was jovial, but there was an underlying edge to it.

"Oh, Ted," Aunt Liz said with a little laugh. "No one thinks that."

"Oh, yeah? You should hear Joe in the New York office when I call him with our daily account information. 'All that noise of the grass growing keeping you up at night, Ted?' He says it almost every day."

"Well, honey, he's probably just jealous."

"Sure, he is. That's why he always mentions some Broadway play he and his wife are going to or some fancy house 'out on the Island' that they're spending the weekend at."

"Oh, Ted," Aunt Liz said again, this time with a sigh.

Sara looked out at the inky darkness all around them. Now and then she'd see a pinpoint of light off in the distance, probably one of the farmhouses they'd seen on the way to the restaurant. The sounds of her aunt and uncle's voices coming from the front seat drifted over her as she slumped against the door and gazed up at a sky still filled with stars. In moments she was asleep.

The next few days were busy ones for Sara. She and her aunt pored over magazines and catalogs, trying to decide what look she wanted for her bedroom. Aunt Liz had zillions of fabric swatches, carpet and wallpaper samples, and paint color charts in the tiny room off the kitchen that she'd converted into her office. As soon as Uncle Ted went to work in the morning, Aunt Liz would drag the stuff out to the dining room and spread it all over the table. Then she and Sara would match up upholstery and drapery fabrics with carpet colors, Aunt Liz muttering things all the while like "too pink," or "that room's too dark for these heavy patterns," or "too stark—you'll get tired of it fast."

Sara had never thought about decorating a room before, at least not like this. Her room at home contained pretty much the same old furniture it had had since she was a kid. A couple of years ago her dad had taken her to a used office-supply store and found a big wood desk that they put in the corner where a glass-fronted hutch full of dolls and toys had stood for as long as she could remember. And not too long ago Sara had purchased a fabulous down comforter on sale when Patti and she had gone shopping with Patti's mom at the May Company. Sara had wanted to bring the comforter with her to Ohio, but her dad had vetoed the idea. He'd said his sister would be insulted, and now Sara could see why.

Finally they decided on some stuff that Sara could see would be really pretty—mossy-green carpet and drapes, a mix of real and reproduction antique furniture, and a pair of down-comforter sets that Sara was sure cost a lot more individually than the one she had at home.

Aunt Liz got busy on the phone with her list of design and color codes. Before long she announced to Sara that almost everything they wanted was in stock and could be delivered within a couple of weeks. By the end of the month Sara's room would be transformed.

"I really appreciate your going to all this trouble for me, Aunt Liz. But isn't this an awful lot of work and money just for one year?" Sara protested.

Her aunt laughed as she gathered everything up off the dining-room table and began storing it back in the room off the kitchen. "Don't be silly, Sara. I'm really happy you're staying with us and I want you to feel at home. It's my pleasure." As Sara handed her the last of the carpet samples to be stowed away, Aunt Liz went on, "You know, your uncle thinks this is just some cute little hobby of mine, something to keep me out of trouble while he's away at work. He doesn't like seeing a mess around. That's why I really try to keep it all put away in here."

Sara looked around the tiny room and guessed that it was originally intended as a place for the washer and dryer. As if reading her thoughts, Aunt Liz said, "I had my carpenter build a new laundry area in the back of the garage. It's just as easy to get to and we certainly didn't need the workbench and tool space that was there before. I don't think Ted would know a Phillips screwdriver if he tripped over one."

Sara laughed. "I didn't think Uncle Ted was the handyman type. But really, Aunt Liz, this room of mine is going to cost you a fortune."

Aunt Liz put her arms around Sara and gave her niece a hug. "Sara, honey, I make money with this little hobby of mine. And I don't have any kids of my own to spend it on, so let me be happy spending it on you, okay?"

Sara looked into the pair of green eyes so like her own, only now clouded with sadness. She wondered why Uncle Ted and Aunt Liz didn't have any children, but she knew this was no time to ask.

CHAPTER 2

The first day of school Sara woke up with a splitting headache. As she washed down two aspirin she looked at herself in the bathroom mirror. Why had she been cursed with hair straight as a stick? She'd inherited her dad's coloring—dark brown, almost black hair, green eyes, and fair skin. But on him the mop of dark curly hair and green eyes gave him an exotic quality. She'd seen the way lots of his female graduate students watched him when he wasn't looking. Even Aunt Liz had pretty hair, curly and dark like Dad's. But Sara had gotten the straight-hair gene from her mom. Except that her mom's hair had been blond!

Sara had decided what she was going to wear to school the night before, but now it looked all wrong. In a frenzy she yanked one top after another out of the closet, discarding them in a heap on the extra bed—too cutesy, too revealing,

too summery, too wintery. Finally she settled
on the outfit that had been her second choice
from the beginning. Aunt Liz was calling her
down to breakfast, but as Sara started out of
her room she looked back at the mess of clothes
on the bed. Uncle Ted didn't like stuff all over
the place, and she certainly didn't want Aunt
Liz cleaning up after her. She started to jam
everything back in the closet, then realized she'd
be back from school long before Uncle Ted got
home from work.

Overton High School was about a mile from
Aunt Liz and Uncle Ted's house. Sara had walked
by the school yesterday afternoon just so she
could make sure she knew the way. But this
morning she was running late and was grateful
when Uncle Ted offered to give her a lift.

Sara's heart was in her throat as they pulled
up in front of the sprawling yellow-brick building. There were mobs of kids hanging around on
the steps and drifting in through the wide double
doors—kids she didn't know. "Go get 'em, tiger,"
Uncle Ted said with a grin. "See you tonight."
Sara gave him what she knew must be a pretty
sickly smile in return and then got out of the car.
As it pulled away she felt totally alone.

Not making eye contact with anyone, Sara
went into the building and looked for the administration office. Aunt Liz had given her good
directions and Sara found her way easily. Noticing the curious glances she was getting, she was

glad that she'd refused Aunt Liz's offer to come with her and help her get registered for class. How embarrassing to have your aunt taking you to school on the first day like a little kid.

But good old Aunt Liz had gotten everything arranged, just like she said she had. Sara was already signed up for her classes, both the required ones and the electives she wanted. Within fifteen minutes she was on her way to her homeroom. As she scurried down the corridor she wondered if her friends at her old school in west Los Angeles would believe it could all be so simple. Of course, there weren't even half as many kids in the whole Overton High School as in just her junior class at home.

Sara raced up the stairs and opened the door to Room 215 just as the morning announcements were being read. Mrs. Lugano, a gray-haired dumpling of a woman, turned to Sara with a smile. "You must be Sara Langdon, our new student from Los Angeles," she said. She indicated an empty desk about halfway back in the third row from the window. Evidently everyone sat in alphabetical order in homeroom.

When she'd finished with the announcements, Mrs. Lugano said they would go through roll call again so that Sara could start getting to know her new classmates. Hating the feeling of being the center of attention but grateful for the teacher's kindness, Sara tried to match faces with names as each student spoke up. But it all seemed to be a blur, and before she knew it, the bell had rung and it was time for first period.

It was the first day of school for everyone else, too, and each student clutched a class schedule, trying to remember where the chemistry room was and busily comparing notes on who had classes with whom. Sara stared at the schedule in her hand; Room 115 was next, and that should be right below the one she was in now. This wasn't going to be so hard.

The pretty blond girl who'd been sitting in the row next to the window came up and smiled. "Hi, Sara. So who do you have first period?" Before Sara could respond, the girl looked over Sara's schedule with a practiced eye and answered for her. "Mr. Wright for English. Great, me too. Come on."

They started down the corridor, Sara trailing after the girl and wishing she could remember her name. At the top of the stairs a big, athletic-looking guy cut across the hall to intercept them. "Hey, Julie. So are you going to be our new junior senator or what?" he asked.

Julie shrugged. "We'll see. Oh, Rick, this is Sara. She's new. From Los Angeles."

As Julie turned away to talk to another guy who'd come up, Rick looked Sara over like a rancher at a cattle auction. "L.A., huh? So, do you hang around with a bunch of movie stars, or what?" Sarcasm dripped from his words as his eyes worked their way up and down her body.

Sara tilted her chin up defiantly. "Sure. My whole life there is just like you see on 'Beverly Hills 90210.' " She didn't like hearing the snotty tone in her voice, but what right had he to leer at her like that?

Reacting to the putdown, Rick sneered. "Hope you've got a lot of memories to keep you warm, 'cause you're not going to see any parties like that around here. In fact, you might not be seeing any parties, period." Ostentatiously giving Sara a dismissive look, he turned on his heel and called to the other girl, "See ya around, Julie."

Sara could feel a flush spreading up her neck and over her cheeks. Luckily Julie was deep in conversation with the other guy and had missed the unpleasant exchange. Suddenly the blond girl said, "Oh, my gosh, we're gonna be late for English. Gotta run, Mike." Then, as an afterthought, she added, "Oh, this is Sara. She's new. From L.A."

Mike smiled hello, and Sara saw an open, friendly face, warm brown eyes, and a slightly crooked nose. But before she could open her mouth to say anything, Julie had grabbed her arm and was propelling her down the stairs. "One thing you gotta know about Mr. Wright," Julie told her as they hurried along the lower corridor. "Everyone says he's fair, but he's a real stickler for rules. That means, don't be late for class. Ever."

Another thing Sara quickly learned about Mr. Wright was that he was very organized. As soon as they settled down and got roll call over with, he announced, "This is accelerated English and each of you has the ability to do the course work. And there's a lot of work to be done. A two-to-five-page paper is due every other Friday; papers with any spelling errors will receive an automatic F. All tests are essay questions. We will be reading and discussing at least three different books during the semester." He paused until the groans subsided and then went on. "If any of you is unwilling to put in the time and effort required for this class, see me right after last period today and I'll sign a transfer slip. I expect those of us who meet here tomorrow to be ready to go to work."

Wow, Sara thought. He certainly doesn't pull his punches. She surreptitiously looked around the room and wondered how many of the desks would be vacant by this time tomorrow.

"Now, for today," Mr. Wright continued, "I'd like to see your writing styles as well as find out a little about each of you. So please use the rest of the period to write an essay on what you hope to accomplish during your junior year. Your goals might be scholastic, athletic, personal, practical, spiritual—whatever is important to you. I'm not asking you to bare your souls. On the other hand, you can rest assured that whatever you write will be strictly confidential. I'll return these essays, marked with my comments, on Thursday. Those of you not planning on remaining in this class can pick up your essays Thursday after school during my office hours."

Sara opened up her notebook to a fresh page and pulled the cap off her pen. She wondered if she should be rethinking accelerated English. "Miss Langdon." Mr. Wright's voice cut into her thoughts. "Did you do the summer reading assignment?" Her dumbfounded look must have been sufficient answer, since he went on, "I'll need to speak to you after school." Sara nodded mutely; this was some kind of course.

As soon as the buzzer sounded, signaling the end of the period, there was a mad rush for the door. Sara saw Julie leave surrounded by a group of three or four other girls and she felt unreasonably let down. The little goodbye wave Julie gave her didn't help. Checking her schedule, Sara headed for the door. What did you expect, she scolded herself, that she'd hold your hand and walk you to every class?

However, the day went steadily downhill. Rick was in Sara's American history class and succeeded in getting a few of his friends to ask Sara how many movie stars she knew in L.A. In spite of her efforts to greet the questions and remarks with a friendly smile, she could tell she wasn't winning points with anyone.

Math class went okay, though, and Sara silently thanked the tough math teacher she'd had last year at home for giving her a leg up on this year's work. She had the feeling she was going to need all the help she could get. And by the time Spanish was over, she was definitely ready for lunch.

So far Sara had managed to meet four people from her homeroom in other classes. They all seemed nice enough, but a lot of the kids were treating her like she had green hair or something. At lunch Julie sat surrounded by a bunch of other girls. She waved Sara over and got everyone to scootch down a little so there was room for her to join them. But when Julie introduced her as "Sara from L.A.," it seemed she might just as well have said "Sara from Mars." The other girls gave her looks that she couldn't decipher, said polite hellos, and then jumped back into the conversation they were having before.

From what Sara could gather, student-council elections were coming up and they were planning Julie's campaign to run for junior senator. Marsha, a skinny, serious-faced girl, decided that they all ought to go to her house right after school and make some campaign posters. Julie suggested Sara join them, but Sara shook her head. "Gotta see Mr. Wright after school," she reminded Julie.

Sara had chemistry after lunch, followed by gym. Her last class of the day was her elective.

Aunt Liz had sent her a list of what was available
and Sara had decided to take something called
"Hands-On Economics—The Beginner's Guide to
Financial Management and Investing." Nothing
like that was offered back home, and if it was too
weird, she figured she could switch to speech or
drama at the semester break.

She was pleasantly surprised to find Julie and
a number of other kids from her homeroom taking the class. The instructor was a young no-
nonsense woman named Ms. Brooks, who began
by assuring them that in the field of finances
and investing, women were at least equal to men
in their ability to grasp the basics and develop
insightful investment strategies. "I'm very happy to see so many young women in this class,"
she said. "The only reason many women feel
they're hopeless in the field of finances is that
they've been taught to think that way. Every
family has a 'designated investor,' and in most of
your families I suspect that that's the man of the
house. Even in single-parent homes, it's unusual
to hear moms talk to daughters about income
investments versus growth investments or discuss the difference between stocks and bonds.
This generation has a chance to change all that
and we're going to begin the change right here."

Ms. Brooks picked up a stack of handouts and
passed them out. "This class isn't just theory,"
she went on. "Lots of you have summer or
after-school jobs that earn a little more than

you really need to spend, and I imagine most of you get allowances. In other words, you have income. In addition some of you probably have savings accounts for college or a special trip that either you or your parents contribute to. That means you have assets. We're going to look over our income and outgo, our assets and liabilities, come up with our short- and longer-range financial goals, and then devise ways for our money to grow. It's going to be an exciting semester."

"I'm glad it's going to be an exciting semester for *her*," Julie grumbled to Sara as soon as class was over. "The only reason I'm taking this is because drama, which I really want to get into, is best in spring semester when they do the school play, and everything else I was remotely interested in was already filled."

Sara actually thought the class sounded like fun, but she didn't want to antagonize the only sort-of friend she'd made so far, so she said mildly, "Well, it might end up okay."

"Yeah, maybe," Julie said dubiously. Then she glanced at the clock on the wall and yelped. "Gotta run or I'll miss my ride. See you tomorrow, Sara."

CHAPTER 3

It was almost 3:30 by the time Sara finished talking to Mr. Wright. She'd had to wait while a whole line of kids from her first-period English class got their transfers signed. Mr. Wright didn't want to hear excuses, but each student seemed impelled to explain at length why dropping the class was an absolute necessity due to personal problems and had nothing to do with the student's willingness to do the class assignments. Mr. Wright didn't even pretend to listen, but it still seemed to take forever, and by the time he got to Sara, he wasn't in a very good mood.

"I know it's not your fault," he said, "but the person in administration your aunt talked to should have let her know about the summer reading assignment. All the sophomores know my junior accelerated English class starts right in using a book we've all read thoroughly during the summer. This year's assignment is P. D. James's *An Unsuitable Job for a Woman*. You'll need your own copy so you can mark it up—I think the BookStop still has some. And you'll need to be ready to start discussing it tomorrow. Just skimming through it won't do. We're going to be looking at style and structure as well as character development."

He already had a copy of Sara's transcript on his desk. After looking at it again, he said, "Of course, you can always transfer to the regular English class—I'm sure there's still a section with room in it. You may find it hard to keep up in this class."

Sara knew her grades weren't spectacular. Her dad had already pointed that out a number of times. But she wasn't going to be shut out of a class just because she hadn't read one lousy book. And she sure wasn't going to let this teacher get away with that kind of put-down. She smiled at him sweetly. "Don't worry, Mr. Wright, I'll be prepared tomorrow. I certainly wouldn't want to transfer out of your class—you've made it sound like so much fun."

As she stalked out of the building Sara realized that she'd let what her dad called her muleheaded stubbornness take over. She just hoped the book wasn't too long.

The afternoon had become hot and yucky, and by the time Sara left the BookStop with her purchase, she felt the same way. Naturally the bookstore was not directly on her way back to Aunt Liz's house, so she had an even longer walk than she'd planned. She trudged along the dusty sidewalk all alone, feeling very sorry for herself.

Suddenly Sara got a prickly feeling on the back of her neck; someone was watching her. She looked around nervously. There was no one else walking on the sidewalk, no cars cruising by slowly on the street. Then she heard the tap of a car horn. A dusty gray car parked across the street started up and swung a U-turn to pull up beside her. "Hi, Sara, I thought it was you. Want a ride?"

It was that nice-looking guy Julie had introduced her to this morning—Mike. "Sure," she said with a grin, and hopped in. The minute she'd slammed the door and he started off down the street, all the dire warnings she'd heard all her life—"don't take rides with strangers"—came flooding into Sara's brain. Oh, please, she told herself firmly, this isn't L.A., it's Overton, Ohio. Nothing bad ever happens here.

"Where do you live?" Mike asked her.

After giving him the address, Sara said, "It didn't seem that far until this afternoon."

"Yeah, you looked kind of wilted. I'm surprised heat bothers you, coming from L.A."

"Oh, it's rarely very hot on the west side of L.A. I guess the ocean breeze helps out." Great, Sara thought. First I look wilted—why couldn't I be one of those girls who looks great no matter what? And now we're talking about the weather, of all things. "So, where were you going?"

Mike looked startled. "Going?" he asked. Then he laughed. "Oh, I get it. You thought I was parked in front of my house. But I wasn't—I'm on my way home too. I live out on the edge of town. I was just stopping by Jeff's to take a look at the campaign posters we're putting up tomorrow." He glanced over at Sara's puzzled expression and went on to explain. "You know, for student council."

"You mean you're running against Julie?" Sara asked.

Mike laughed. "Gosh, no, seniors don't run against juniors. Each grade votes for its own two senators. I hope Julie and I both win. She'll be good in student government."

Sara was still silently digesting the fact that Mike was a senior as they pulled up in front of her house. She'd hoped that maybe he was interested in her when he offered to give her a ride, but now she realized that he was just being nice to the new kid at school. "Thanks for the lift," she told him. "If I were a senior, you'd have my vote!"

He grinned. "Great. I hope everyone feels that way!"

As Mike zoomed off Aunt Liz opened the front door and came out on the porch. "From what I could tell, he's pretty cute. I guess you did okay for your first day at a new school."

"The ride was the only okay thing about today. And that's all it was—a ride. And now I've got about a million hours of homework plus a whole book to read," Sara said with a sigh.

Aunt Liz gave her a hug. "Tomorrow's bound to be better. Come on in the kitchen and get a snack to help you with your studies. And I hope you like chicken curry, 'cause that's what we're having for dinner."

The tantalizing odor of curry wafted up the stairs, and by the time Aunt Liz called her to dinner, Sara was starving. At the table she caught herself considering a third helping and wondered what it was about this place that made her so hungry. Whatever it was, she'd better get over it soon or she'd be big as a house by Halloween. She could go trick-or-treating as an extra-plump Pillsbury dough girl and not need any padding. Sara giggled at the image.

"What's so funny?" Uncle Ted asked with a slight edge to his voice.

"Oh, nothing. I was just thinking about how fat I'm going to be if you guys keep feeding me these great meals."

Uncle Ted's face cleared. "You're right. This is terrific curry, Liz." He said to Sara, "You don't know how lucky you are. Your aunt is usually so busy running around all involved in those little jobs she does that I figured we might as well buy stock in frozen-food companies and takeout joints."

"Well, I wanted to be around while Sara's getting settled in. But don't you two get too used to this domestic stint, because I think I landed another job today."

"That's great, Aunt Liz. Good for you," Sara said enthusiastically.

Uncle Ted gave them both a sardonic smile. "Busy, busy," he commented.

Ignoring his gentle mockery, Aunt Liz warned, "It might involve a buying trip or two. But that won't be for a while. So enjoy home-cooked food while you can."

During the next two days Sara saw the evidence of lots of campaign activity. The school elections were only a couple of weeks away and every available wall had a campaign poster on it. The whole school took the student-council elections seriously. Each grade was represented by two senators and each homeroom got to elect one representative. The senators and representatives, along with the elected school president, vice-president, secretary, and treasurer, formed the student council. They met every week to discuss school policies and to plan school events. In addition, the senators formed the student disciplinary board and could recommend detention or even suspension.

Sara got involved in Julie's campaign, hoping that it would be a good way to meet people. At lunch on Thursday, Julie wolfed down her cafeteria-style tuna surprise as she came up with one campaign idea after another, discarding each of them in turn. Suddenly Sara said, "Why not make campaign bookmarks and give them away to all the kids in the junior class? They could say something like 'Julie Baker marks the spot' or 'Know where you're at with Julie Baker.' What do you think?"

Julie stared at Sara in amazement. "I think it sounds terrific. But won't it cost a fortune?"

Sara shook her head. "All we have to do is design one. Then we can copy the design five times on one sheet of paper. If we made about twenty copies of that one page, we could cut them up into enough for the whole junior class. I'll see if my uncle can run off copies on his office machine—we could do them on colored construction paper."

Julie grinned at Sara and then turned to the other girls who were just joining them at the table. "You guys are not going to believe what a fabulous idea my new campaign manager came up with! Sara, tell them all about it!"

By lunchtime the next day, Sara realized that she hadn't done too badly for her first week in a new school. Lots of kids said hi to her in the halls, classes were going okay, and she could look forward to a place saved just for her at one of the best lunch tables. Julie had really been a pal to include her in so much, and the two of them were becoming real friends.

Everything was going well with Julie's election campaign, and Sara was surprised at the long faces that greeted her when she got to the cafeteria. "What's up?" she asked.

"Oh, my gosh, I guess you haven't heard," LuAnn Philips said in a tragic voice. "Marlene Marrs was raped last night. She was working late down at the Pit Stop—I guess you don't know her 'cause she graduated last year, but when she was getting into her car, this guy in a ski mask attacked her."

Sara was stunned. How could something so awful happen in this seemingly peaceful little town?

"It's got to be the same guy from last year." Marsha said what they were all thinking. "Everyone figured he left the area, but I guess we were wrong."

"You mean there was another rape here last year?" Sara asked.

"Oh, yeah, two," LuAnn told her.

"Both times last year it was some guy wearing one of those knitted ski masks, so the girls who were raped couldn't see his face," Julie explained. "Last night's rape sounds just like what happened before, so everyone thinks it must be the same man."

Watching Sara's expression of mounting horror, LuAnn couldn't help adding, "And last spring Mary Jo Rice disappeared. She was a senior and nobody knows what ever happened to her."

Sara gasped, but before she could say anything, a girl named Shari chimed in. "Well, I don't know about Mary Jo—she was kind of a

loner and maybe she just ran away. But those
other two were definitely raped by the ski-mask
guy."

"Yeah, and this time they're gonna get him.
My dad told me they've got evidence." Seeing
Sara's puzzled expression, LuAnn added, "My
dad's a cop."

The rest of the day everyone at school seemed
strangely quiet. Kids kept together in groups
and the normal hilarity that marked the end
of a Friday at school and the beginning of the
weekend was missing. Sara stayed after school
to help Julie and LuAnn rehang some of the posters, and then the three of them wandered out to
the football field to watch the team tryouts.

It was a gorgeous fall afternoon and a bunch
of other students were sprawled on the bleachers
catching a few rays while the team sweated on
the field. "That's Mike isn't it? Number forty-
four?" Sara asked. "I didn't know he was trying
out for the football team."

LuAnn looked at Sara in amazement. "Are you
kidding? Mike doesn't need to try out for the
team. Last year he made more touchdowns than
anybody else. Practically broke the league record."

A few minutes later the players took a short
break and Mike jogged over to where the three
girls were standing. "Hi," he said. "You guys gonna hang around awhile?"

Julie and LuAnn shook their heads. "Can't.

Got stuff to do," they said almost in unison.

"What about you, Sara?" he asked.

Sara shrugged, feeling totally tongue-tied.

Mike seemed not to notice. "Well, if you're still here when we're done, I'll give you a ride home," he told her, and then jogged back to join his teammates.

A little while later Julie and LuAnn decided they'd better get going. "I guess I don't have to worry about how Sara's getting home," LuAnn said to Julie.

Sara felt a red flush start at the back of her neck. "It's just a ride," she said in embarrassment.

"Sure," Julie said with a grin. Then her face became serious. "Just make sure you do get that ride. One tragedy around here is enough."

"Don't worry," Sara told her. But as soon as the other girls left, she was absorbed in watching Mike play, the rape of poor Marlene Marrs far from her mind.

By the time they got to Sara's house it was almost six. As Mike pulled up, Aunt Liz came rushing out of the house. "Sara, honey, where have you been?" she asked. "I've been so worried about you."

It's still broad daylight out, Sara thought. At home her dad never got unglued about her staying late after school. But Aunt Liz didn't have kids of her own, Sara reminded herself. Maybe her aunt was just a little overprotective. Hastily

Sara explained where she'd been and introduced Mike.

Uncle Ted's car pulled into the driveway and he got out with a scowl on his face. Reluctantly he shook hands with Mike and then abruptly went into the house. Mike took off, and when Sara and Aunt Liz got inside, Uncle Ted was still scowling.

"Who is that kid, anyway? What does he do?" Uncle Ted asked Sara.

"Do? He doesn't do anything. I mean, he goes to school. Mike's a real nice guy, Uncle Ted. He's on the football team and student council and . . ." Sara trailed off. Student council wasn't exactly the truth, but everyone was sure he was going to win.

"Oh, great, a jock who drives a beat-up car. I don't want you to have anything to do with him," Uncle Ted told her.

Sara was about to protest. Who was Uncle Ted to tell her what to do? And how dare he make that kind of snap judgment based on the kind of car a person drove? But before she could open her mouth, she felt Aunt Liz's warning hug around her shoulders. "Ted, why don't you go up and change and then we'll have cocktails on the back patio. It's such a pretty evening."

As Uncle Ted disappeared up the stairs Aunt Liz said to Sara, "Your uncle's had a hard week at work and he's kind of grumpy. He'll feel differently by tomorrow. But, honey, you did give me a scare. With that rape and all, I just didn't know what to think."

While Aunt Liz continued talking about how upset everyone was, Sara thought, Boy, news travels fast in Los Angeles, but here it moves like lightning. Every soul in Overton must have heard all the details of last night's rape. Sara felt even sorrier for Marlene Marrs. How awful it must be to live in a little town like this and know that every person you see has been talking about what happened to you.

"She probably asked for it." Uncle Ted was coming back downstairs, having changed out of his suit and tie.

"How can you say such a thing! She was at work, like any regular person. She wasn't the one who did something wrong!" Sara realized she was shouting. "No one asks to be raped," she said in a quieter tone.

"Well, what kind of girl works at a drive-in? Answer me that," Ted said dismissively. "Come on, Liz. Where are those drinks? I'm sure ready for one. Sara, you joining us?"

"No. I've got homework." Sara pressed her lips together before she said more and then ran up the stairs.

CHAPTER 4

Julie called Sara later that evening. "So, did he ask you out?" she wanted to know.

For a moment the question didn't make any sense; Sara's mind was still back in time with the leaders of the American Revolution that she'd been studying for history class. Then she laughed. "Oh, you mean Mike."

"No, I meant Rocky the Flying Squirrel. Of course, I'm talking about Mike. Well?"

Sara sighed, and hearing that as an answer, Julie sighed with her. "I don't think he's really interested in me," Sara said. "I think he's just being nice because I'm new in town."

"Right," Julie told her. "That's Mike all right. Mr. Nice Guy. Yep. He's given rides home to every new kid who's ever moved to Overton. In fact, just last month he got a medal for being so thoughtful."

"Oh, you know what I mean," Sara said. "He

probably feels sorry for me because I don't know anyone yet."

"Thanks a lot. So now I've become a nobody."

"Oh, Julie, I didn't mean you. It's just that all you guys have known each other practically since you were born. You've all done stuff together forever, your families have done stuff together forever—I don't even have a real family here."

"Oh, excuse me while I weep for you," Julie said in mock disgust. "Come off it, Sara. You just got here. What do you expect?"

Sara laughed. "I'm really lucky to have you as a friend, Julie. What would I do without you?"

"I like the sound of that—maybe I can use something about friends for my speech about why I should be elected junior-class senator. I mean, I've got to come up with some grabby issues or something, or I won't have a chance of winning."

After a moment Sara said slowly, "I think you should talk to the kids in our homeroom—they seem to be kind of left out of this whole election and maybe they have some ideas no one else will think of."

"I don't know those kids very well," Julie replied doubtfully. "They're not exactly a bunch of nerds, but a lot of them are such serious students, I'm not sure if . . ." She trailed off.

"You could give it a try," Sara told her. "It can't hurt."

"Don't you think they'll figure out I'm just

buttering them up to get votes?" Julie asked.

"Well, if that's what you're planning on doing, sure they will. But most people like to be asked what they think about stuff, and it's an opportunity for you to look at things from a different perspective."

"When you're right, you're right," Julie said. "But, Sara, you have to help me out on this. A lot of kids might be more willing to talk to you because you're new—you don't have a bunch of preconceived ideas."

"Okay," Sara said uncertainly, wondering what she'd gotten herself into.

"Good!" Julie exclaimed. "Now about tomorrow . . ." They confirmed their plans to go to the mall and then Sara returned to the American Revolution. Before long she turned off her light and slid into bed.

Three hours later the house was quiet, and outside, the glow of the moon disappeared and reappeared as lazy clouds shuttled across the sky. But inside Sara's head all was violent confusion. The night lights and sounds of the carnival seemed distorted and amplified. Game barkers reached out, grasping at her sleeves, and shouted at her to take a chance. She ran, stumbling over the rutted dirt fairground, past the gypsy fortune-teller, past the merry-go-round with horses that neighed and stomped their feet. The entrance to the fun house was just ahead of her and she raced through its portal, not stopping to buy a ticket. Skeletons jumped out at her, bats caught their feet in her hair.

Sara glanced back over her shoulder. Her breath was coming in little gasps now. But the man in the ski mask loped tirelessly along behind her. Was there no escape? Then she saw the entrance to a tiny room and ran inside it to hide. The room filled with blue light, and suddenly there he was right in front of her, the man in the ski mask. His hands reached out for her as Sara backed away screaming.

Just before the man's hands touched her, Sara woke up with a start. Her heart was pounding and her body was drenched in sweat. She looked wildly around the room and then shook her head, trying to rid herself of the fear she still felt. Gradually her pulse slowed and her body relaxed. It was just a scary dream, she told herself. Go back to sleep.

But that turned out to be more easily decided than done. Every time Sara closed her eyes, the images of the frightening dream returned. Finally she climbed out of bed and got a glass of water from the bathroom. Then she settled down under the covers with the bedside lamp on and her American history text in her lap. As she tried to absorb the details of the Continental Congress, Sara found her eyes drooping and before long she slid into uninterrupted sleep.

Sara slept in late that Saturday morning and awoke tired and cranky, but by noon she was so happy she felt she could fly. Mike had called and asked if she wanted to go to a movie with him that night. Sara said yes and hung up the phone before she even thought about asking Aunt Liz and Uncle Ted if it was okay. Well, it would just have to be. She was used to making her own plans at home in L.A. and she didn't see why anything had to be different here in Overton. Nevertheless, as she raced out of the house when Julie honked the horn, a voice of concern began to nag at the back of her mind.

Aunt Liz had been very firm about Sara not going anywhere alone until the rapist had been caught. And that wasn't a problem; everyone else's parents had said the same thing. Still, Sara didn't know what she was going to do about her date that night with Mike. Going to the movies with him certainly wasn't going out alone, but what was Uncle Ted going to say? Sara realized that she was counting on Aunt Liz to figure something out. Aunt Liz was okay.

Julie sat behind the wheel of her mom's station wagon waiting for Sara to hop in. Sara felt the same lump of envy she did whenever she saw one of her girlfriends driving. Why did her birthday have to be so late in the year? Absolutely everyone she knew was already sixteen and driving. Sara knew how to drive and she was sure she'd pass her test with no problem. Besides, Dad had told Aunt Liz it was okay for Sara to get her license. But would Uncle Ted object? Sara sighed. She hoped her uncle's overprotective attitude would start to loosen up soon.

At the mall Sara and Julie saw lots of other kids from school. Just as they were going toward the food section they ran into Melodie Burton and Ginger Swift, two girls that Julie sometimes hung around with. But instead of suggesting that they all have lunch together, Julie pretended that she and Sara were leaving and waited until she saw the other two enter a shop before quickly dragging Sara into the food hall. "What was that about?" Sara wanted to know.

"Oh, I thought I'd rather have lunch in peace instead of being in the middle of a food fight," Julie told her. "I guess you don't know that Melodie hates your guts."

"What?" Sara was astounded. "I thought she liked me."

"She probably did. Before you snatched her boyfriend." As Sara opened her mouth in surprise Julie raised a pacifying hand and went on. "I know you didn't know Mike and Melodie were going together, and the reason is that they weren't. At least not this year. But they were an item last year before Mel got all excited about this college guy who came home for the summer. Then, of course, she dumped Mike so fast he didn't know what was happening."

"So what's her problem with me, then, if she dumped him?"

"Simple. The college guy went back to school."

"And now Melodie wants Mike back?"

"Right." Julie nodded. "But Mike's not interested. He's not a total dope."

"I still don't see where I fit into all this," Sara said around a mouthful of salad.

"You're in the way. At least that's how Melodie sees it. Or maybe she just feels that if she can't have him, no one else can. All I'm telling you is, watch out."

Later that afternoon Sara told her aunt about the date with Mike that night. "I don't know why Uncle Ted doesn't like him," she said.

"I don't know either, honey," her aunt confided. "Sometimes I just haven't got a clue about where your uncle's coming from. Don't worry, though, I'm sure it will work out. Mike seems like a nice boy."

Mike came into the house to pick Sara up and she made sure she was ready when he got there. She didn't want to leave him alone with Uncle Ted. Just as she'd suspected, her uncle was there opening the door and asking Mike who his dad was and what he did for a living before Mike even got inside. Doing her best to smile disarmingly at her uncle, Sara hustled Mike and herself out the door; she didn't want to give Uncle Ted time to cross-examine him further. "I'm really sorry about that," she told Mike as she settled into the front seat.

Mike shrugged it off. Everyone had problems with parents, so it just figured that an uncle would be even worse. "They've all got something they're crazed about," he told her. "Maybe it's midlife crisis or something. My dad doesn't care who I hang out with or what I do so long as I keep making touchdowns."

"So how do you plan to manage schoolwork and student council and football too?" Sara asked.

Mike shrugged again. "I'll work it out. Student council is something I really want to do. If something's going to suffer it'll probably be my grades. I just need to do well enough to stay on the team. My dad's sure I'm going to get a football scholarship. He wants me to be a pro."

"What do you want?" Sara asked softly.

"Oh, I don't know. See, my dad hurt his knee when he was just starting out in the pros. His career was washed up, but he figures I'll make up for it."

As Mike parked the car in the lot behind Overton's elderly single-screen theater, he apologized for not taking Sara to the new multiplex in the mall. "The movie I wanted to see isn't at the mall," he explained. Then he looked at her with apprehension. "Guess this isn't like going to the movies in L.A.," he said. "Overton must seem like pretty small potatoes to you."

Sara smiled up at him. "Oh, it's got its compensations."

After the movie Sara and Mike went to Jake's, the pizza place just outside of town. It was obviously the local teen hangout and soon the two of them were surrounded by Mike's buddies and their dates.

As they walked outside the sky was again filled with stars. Mike took hold of Sara's hand and she felt a little shiver of excitement. That Melodie was really a fool, she decided as Mike pulled her close for a brief, tantalizing kiss. "I'd better get you home," he said. His voice sounded husky. "That uncle of yours is just the kind to wait up for you, and I don't want to get on his bad side any more than I already am."

Julie called Sara the next day to find out how her date with Mike was. They agreed to meet in the park so Sara could talk without her aunt and uncle hanging around to listen. Mike had been right; Uncle Ted had been waiting up for her to come home the night before. Sara thought it made her look like a little kid, and she didn't enjoy the feeling.

That night after dinner Sara was loading the dishwasher while her aunt packaged the leftovers and put them in the refrigerator. Uncle Ted was watching "60 Minutes" in the living room. "It's not that I mind doing the dishes, Aunt Liz," Sara said, "but how come Uncle Ted never helps you at all? Doesn't he usually do anything like clear the table?"

Her aunt laughed shortly. "Ted? Oh, no." Then in a gentler tone she told Sara, "Your uncle has some pretty old-fashioned ideas about what's 'men's work' and what women are supposed to do. He figures that he's at work all day earning enough to keep us in comfort and he's entitled to enjoy himself when he's home."

Sara gaped at her in amazement. "He actually says stuff like that?"

Aunt Liz reached up to smooth a strand of dark hair away from Sara's face. Her touch was soft and kind. "I know it must seem odd to you, honey, but really I don't mind. It's just his way. Ted is very generous to me, and we have a lot of fun together sometimes. Besides, he takes care of all the bills and stuff like that, and you know, keeping accounts in order is quite a bit of work too."

"Right. And poor helpless little you wouldn't know how to do all that account keeping," Sara said, her voice heavy with sarcasm. "But somehow you're able to run your own business and keep all _those_ accounts and order stuff and keep workmen in line and like that."

As soon as the words were out of her mouth, Sara was sorry. There wasn't any need to sound so snotty. After all, it was pretty nice of Uncle Ted to welcome his wife's niece into his home for a whole year, even though it must be causing a lot of changes in his everyday routine.

But Aunt Liz just smiled. "Oh, Sara, give your uncle a little credit. The money my little business makes is mine to do with as I please," she said. "And speaking of that, I'm going to be out of town for a couple of days this week, so let me show you what I've fixed for you two to have for dinner." She led Sara over to the freezer and opened the door. There were stacks of plastic containers, all neatly labeled. "There's plenty of this lasagna for you to have a friend over if you want. And I made enough chili for an army."

"When did you do all this?" Sara wanted to know. She'd never seen a freezer so well stocked with homemade goodies.

"Well, I've been using the time when you're at school and Ted's at work to good advantage this past week. Now your uncle may decide to eat out with friends from work some nights, but unless he tells you he's not coming home for dinner, if you could just defrost something and put together a salad and a vegetable or potatoes when I'm not here, I'd really appreciate it. Ted always likes to sit down to a home-cooked dinner."

"Hey, Aunt Liz, no problem," Sara told her with a smile. "This is gourmet heaven. Nothing's ever this easy at home."

"Oh, thanks so much, Sara. I was sure I could count on you. I'll leave my schedule posted here on the refrigerator door so you'll know what's happening in advance."

Sara gave her aunt a hug. "Like I said, it's no big deal. I'm used to cooking at home all the time. But what happens when I'm not living here?"

"Oh, I usually try very hard not to be gone in the evenings. The few times I have, your uncle grumbled so much that the business I got almost wasn't worth it." She hugged her niece back. "So you see, I'm taking advantage of your being here. I hope it really is okay."

Sara assured her aunt once again that it was perfectly fine, but on her way up to her room to study she couldn't help thinking that if anyone was taking advantage, it was Uncle Ted.

CHAPTER 5

The next two weeks at school seemed to fly by. Once Mr. Wright had scared away almost a third of the original accelerated English class with his tough approach, he turned out to be a pussycat. He worked almost as hard as his students did on their weekly essays, and much to Sara's relief, he gave everyone more slack with the reading assignments than they'd expected. At his suggestion, Sara and Julie teamed up and proofread each other's essays, with the result that writing the papers was easier for both of them.

The other class that Sara and Julie shared, Hands-On Economics, was more of a problem. While Sara enjoyed making up a budget and filling in all the expenditures for the mythical family the class was tracking, Julie couldn't see the point. "I don't get it," she told Sara one afternoon while they were sprawled in Sara's room working on the assignment. "I mean, when you see you're going to run out of money, you just have to slow down the spending. What's the point of all these charts and lists? It's all just common sense."

Sara shrugged. "Maybe when we get involved in the investing part you'll find it more interesting. Remember what Ms. Brooks was saying about using the Rule of Seventy-two to figure out how fast your money will double?"

"Yeah, sure," Julie said with a sigh. "The way I look at it we could be millionaires by the time we're sixty-five, but by then we'd be too old to enjoy it."

Sara laughed. Her friend had a point.

Meanwhile Sara spent a fair amount of time talking to kids from Mrs. Lugano's homeroom about what they wanted student council to do in the coming year. At first she felt shy talking to kids she didn't know, but it turned out that having a purpose for the conversations made things a lot easier. She was making friends and at the same time she was learning quite a bit about her new school.

And, Sara thought, things were going well with Mike. She still didn't feel she knew him very well, but he was a lot of fun to be with. And she couldn't help being flattered that the star of the Overton football team wanted to go out with her.

On the days that Mike didn't have football practice after school he gave Sara a ride home. The rest of the time he would have been happy to have her wait for practice to end, but that would have meant that they'd arrive at Sara's almost the same time Uncle Ted did. Her uncle made no bones about thinking that Mike wasn't good enough for Sara to be seeing, so she tried to avoid confrontations between the two of them as much as she could, and so far it seemed to be working.

In fact, everything was going really well, Sara thought—except for Rick Black. Ever since that little run-in Sara had had with him on her first day at school, Rick couldn't stop trying to get her to explode. He baited her with sly remarks about "L.A. airheads" and "movie-star groupies" and people who thought they were better than anyone else. Sara tried to ignore him, but it was hard.

One day as she was walking out of American history, she heard Rick say from behind her, "Hey, Sara, I've been wondering—are you sure you're from L.A.? I thought all the girls out there were blond and beautiful."

Keeping her eyes resolutely focused on the door in front of her, Sara continued walking. Then she heard another voice.

"Oh, Rick, grow up. Are you so desperate for attention from a girl? You sound like my nine-year-old cousin." It was Diane Wallace, who sat near Sara in history and sometimes ate lunch with Julie's group. She came up beside Sara and said loudly, "Aren't these little boys boring?"

Then the two of them walked down the hall,
leaving Rick glowering behind them.

Sara had been so grateful to Diane. She could
never think of anything to say herself that would
shut Rick up. It was a little surprising to see normally quiet Diane be so brave, and so quick with
a cutting remark. After Diane's put-down, Rick
was careful not to torment Sara when Diane was
around—but he still made sly digs whenever he
found an opportunity.

When they weren't studying, Sara and Julie
spent all their time together working on Julie's
campaign and the speech she would give to the
whole school. Sara's idea of surveying the kids
in their own homeroom was paying off. In addition to getting some good ideas of what issues
were important to juniors, Julie gathered a lot
of support from a group she didn't normally
hang around with. By the end of the second
week everyone in Mrs. Lugano's homeroom was
actively campaigning for Julie.

All the pre-election excitement, as well as the
normal demands of homework and social life,
kept kids from dwelling on Marlene Marrs's
rape. Of course the parents' rules for girls not
going out by themselves were still pretty much
in effect. And every now and then one of Julie
and Sara's friends mentioned seeing Marlene in
town and then the whole lunch group would
spend some time talking about how awful it
was, and LuAnn Philips would pass on whatever

she'd heard from her policeman father. But the pressures of everyday life soon became the focus of conversation again.

Sara hadn't had any more bad dreams about the man in the ski mask since that first one, and was grateful. She had enough other things to think about without some crazy rapist chasing her in her sleep.

Monday was election day. There would be an all-school assembly during last period, when all the candidates for senator and for the officers would give their speeches. After that the students would cast their votes. During homeroom that morning Mrs. Lugano barely controlled the bedlam as Julie was peppered with questions and advice about her forthcoming speech. Suddenly Dick Stone, the homeroom's computer whiz, said, "In all the excitement trying to get Julie elected as class senator, we haven't even talked about who's going to run as our homeroom representative. Maybe we'd better give that some thought—the election is this afternoon."

The room became quiet as the students looked around at one another. Slowly Sara raised her hand. "Maybe Dick should do it. He's the one who brought it up, and besides, he's pretty forceful when he wants to win an argument." Everyone laughed; Dick Stone was captain of the school's debating team. He spent time thinking things through, and once he'd made up his mind, he was almost unbeatable.

Dick looked a little embarrassed and shrugged. But before he could say anything, Julie blurted out, "Why not elect Sara? She's a hard worker, and besides, she's really made an effort to find out how everyone in the homeroom feels about lots of different issues. She'd do a great job of representing us!"

This time it was Sara's turn to look embarrassed. She had never understood how anyone could run for office and get up and toot his own horn over and over. She admired Julie's ability to keep her own campaign going without an abundance of self-admiration. And while Sara felt she probably would be able to represent her homeroom well, she wasn't sure that it was fair for her to be in student government when she'd only be in the school one year.

Mrs. Lugano tapped a piece of chalk on the board to bring order to the buzzing conversation that had erupted in the room. "We have two nominations so far—Dick Stone and Sara Langdon. Are there any others?" She looked around at the roomful of silent faces. "All right, then. Do I hear seconds to these nominations?"

Several people spoke up to second Dick and Sara, but Sara was too flustered to notice who they were. Then Mrs. Lugano asked Sara and Dick if they agreed to run and they both gave her shy nods.

"Fine. We have two candidates for our homeroom representative to the student council. As you know, all voting will be done this afternoon following the assembly. But since homeroom candidates don't speak at the assembly, perhaps each of you would like to make a short statement now."

Sara felt her whole neck and face turn hot and she knew she was bright red to the roots of her hair. Luckily Mrs. Lugano called on Dick to speak first. He got up from his desk and slowly walked to the front of the room.

"I'm not really prepared to make a speech," he began with a grin. "But since most of you have known me since before kindergarten, there's probably nothing I could say that would change your minds about me anyway." He laughed along with the rest of the class. Then his expression grew more serious. "However, I feel I can do a good job of representing all of you. I've seen the problems we have at Overton High, and if elected, I think I can find solutions for them." Dick grinned again. "I just wish that someone other than my opponent had nominated me. Thank you." He sat down to whistles and applause, and then everyone quieted down as Sara stood up.

During the walk to the front of the room that was at the same time unbearably long and incredibly short, Sara wished that she could crawl into a hole and pull it in after her. Dick was used to speaking on his feet; he had managed to be both funny and serious in those few words and he had a politician's easy manner. She just hoped she wouldn't make a total fool of herself.

"As you all know, I'm new to Overton High this year, and so what I have to offer is inexperience." Sara smiled shyly and then went on. "But inexperience isn't always a bad thing. It allows me to look at Overton High with a fresh eye. It also ensures that I will ask you about issues and not assume I know how you feel. Being part of student government is a responsibility and an honor. If elected, I will represent this homeroom and everyone in it to the best of my ability. Thank you."

There was a moment of silence when Sara finished and then the room broke into another round of thunderous applause. Mrs. Lugano again rapped on the chalkboard for order. "We are indeed fortunate to have two wonderful candidates for homeroom representative." She smiled at Sara and Dick. "Now, please come back here this afternoon immediately after the assembly so that you can pick up your ballots and vote."

The buzzer announced the end of homeroom period and there was a general shuffling of books and papers as the students scrambled out of their desks and headed for the door. Sara scurried out as fast as she could, but Julie caught up with her in the hall and gave her a big hug. "You did great! You're going to win for sure," she told her friend. "I just hope I can sound half as put together this afternoon."

Sara was still too shaken to respond, so she gave Julie a weak smile and then watched her pretty blond friend hurry off to her next class, smiling and yelling hi to other students as she went. Julie's so great with people, Sara thought. Her friendliness and outgoing manner made her popular, but it was her natural kindness that made her really well liked. The campaign for Julie's election was going very well and Sara was confident that her friend would win. But she certainly didn't feel the same about her own chances.

The rest of the day went by in a kind of haze for Sara. Some kids from her homeroom stopped her in the halls to say they were voting for her; others breezed by and said nothing, from which Sara gathered that their preference was for Dick. She wanted to talk to Mike, but every time she saw him he was huddled with his buddies, and it looked like they were working over last-minute campaign strategies.

By the time the all-school assembly started, Sara was still feeling totally ambiguous about the election she'd unexpectedly become involved in. On the one hand, being on student council would be interesting and a lot of fun. She'd never have a chance to do something like this in Los Angeles, where the school was so much bigger and homerooms didn't have their own representatives. So, of course, she couldn't help hoping.

On the other hand, Dick was a known quantity with the kids who were voting. While Sara had tried to make her newness seem like an advantage, she wasn't sure she'd buy that argument herself. And Dick was a smart guy who'd do a good job. As she settled into her seat in the auditorium, Sara decided to put the whole thing out of her mind. There was nothing she could do about it at this point anyway.

The assembly began with speeches from the kids who were nominated for president, vice-president, secretary, and treasurer of student council. Then came those running for class senator, starting with the seniors. There were four besides Mike, and while all of them had worked hard on their campaigns, three of the five were doomed to disappointment tomorrow morning. Sara hoped that everyone felt as she did that Mike's speech was the best. It wasn't the most polished, but his caring and sincerity shone through. Surely he'll win, she thought. He's really popular and he's worked hard on his campaign—he wants to be on student council. But Sara knew that hard work and caring didn't always win the prize.

Julie gave an excellent speech, bringing up a number of issues that Sara had recommended, based on conversations with the kids in their homeroom. Afterward a crowd of students

swarmed around her with congratulations and
Sara couldn't even get close. She went over
to where Mike was standing surrounded by
most of the football team. When he spotted
her, he reached through the mob of big guys
and pulled her close in a hug.

"You were really great," Sara told him, her
eyes shining.

Mike grinned. "Thanks. I sure hope lots of other people feel the same way." Then he bent down
and said softly, "I really want to be with you,
but the coach is insisting that this afternoon is
practice as usual. Can you believe it? And then I
told the guys who helped me out on my campaign
that we'd all go out for pizza."

"That's okay," Sara whispered. "We'll have a
victory celebration tomorrow."

Mike gave her waist another squeeze. "You're
on!"

A loud microphone announcement rang out,
reminding everyone to get back to their homerooms on the double and vote. Sara gave Mike
another big smile and a thumbs-up for victory
and then headed into the hall along with about
a million other kids. She didn't see Julie until
they were practically at the homeroom door.

As soon as Julie spotted Sara, she wormed
her way over to her. "We're a winning team,
partner. I've got my fingers crossed for both of
us," she said, grabbing Sara's hand and crossing
Sara's own fingers also. Silently Sara crossed the

fingers on her other hand—good luck for Mike,
too, she hoped.

It was oddly quiet during the homeroom voting, as if talking to one candidate would hurt the
other one's feelings. Almost before Sara knew it,
she and Julie were back out in the hall again, the
voting over and nothing to do but wait until the
next morning when the winners would be posted
on the school bulletin board.

"My mom said I could drive her car to school
today," Julie told Sara. "So let's go to the mall.
Practically the whole school will be there anyway. And I'm so wound up I can hardly sit still.
But you know that shopping always calms me
down," she added with a wicked grin. "A bunch
of us will probably get some pizza and then we
can catch a movie if it's not too late."

"But . . ." What about homework? What about
Uncle Ted's dinner? she thought.

As if reading her mind, Julie said, "Don't sweat
the homework. Didn't you notice that everyone
gave out real Mickey Mouse assignments today?
None of the teachers expects anything will get
done tonight. It's a school tradition."

Sara was really tempted to take the afternoon
and evening off, but Aunt Liz was out of town and
Sara had promised to take care of feeding Uncle
Ted while she was gone. When she explained her
problem, Julie laughed. "That's no big deal," she
assured Sara. "We'll stop by your house on the
way to the mall. It won't take us ten minutes to

pull something out of the freezer, make a salad, and set the table. We can write him a note telling him how high to set the oven and how long it needs to cook. Even my dad can turn on the oven and he's a real Neanderthal—your uncle Ted can't be any more incapable than my dad."

"Sounds like a plan to me," Sara said enthusiastically. "I'll give him a call from the house and tell him what we're doing and that the two of us will be safe and sound together. He'll probably be thrilled to hear that I'm out with you instead of Mike!"

When they got there, Sara called her uncle while Julie rummaged in the freezer. As soon as she put down the phone, Sara yelled, "You can forget the foraging. Uncle Ted's going to be out tonight anyway."

Julie slammed the freezer door. "He wasn't mad, was he?" she asked anxiously, and suddenly Sara realized that at least part of Julie's easygoing manner was really bravado.

It was Sara's turn to be casual. "Not at all. He said he was 'delighted' I was going out with my 'pretty blond girlfriend' and he hoped we'd have a great time."

For a fleeting instant Sara wished that Aunt Liz was home. It would be great to tell her about being nominated for homeroom representative. Then, as she climbed into Julie's mom's car, she thought, Aunt Liz would probably get all excited about it and be on pins and needles all night and all day tomorrow. Then it would be really disappointing to have to tell her I lost. No, it's just as well that Aunt Liz doesn't know and that Julie and I are going out together. They were almost to the mall before Sara realized that it never occurred to her to talk about the elections to Uncle Ted.

CHAPTER 6

The next morning Sara got up extra early and had already wolfed down some cereal and was putting on her jacket by the time her uncle came downstairs in his business suit ready for breakfast. "Hang on a minute," he said to Sara. "Are you off to school already? I was planning to give you a ride. Just hold your horses."

"Thanks anyway, Uncle Ted," Sara said, improvising fast. "But I've got to catch up on some reading I didn't do last night and it'll be better to do it in the school library."

"I can imagine. You got home a little late, didn't you?"

Sara didn't answer. She hated the feeling that Uncle Ted was keeping tabs on her every minute of the day and night, but it wasn't worth causing a big scene.

With a quick goodbye, Sara slipped out of the house and then trotted down the sidewalk. The real reason she wanted to get to school early was so she could see the election results without a whole crowd of kids around her. Sara was all too aware that her face often gave away her feelings, and much as she hated to admit it even to herself, she had spent last night dreaming of three election victories—Mike's, Julie's, and her own. Although she knew she didn't stand a chance, the enthusiasm of the group of girls last night at the pizza place had made anything seem possible. Now, as reality came closer every minute, Sara felt prepared for defeat even though the bubble of hope kept welling up inside her. Whatever happened, she didn't want anyone to know how much she cared.

As she got to the corner across from the front of the school, Sara could see that she was too late. Lots of other students must have been eager to see the election results—dozens of kids hung out on the front steps and wandered in and out of the main door. The bulletin board was right inside.

Quickly Sara began fumbling with her books, pretending she was looking for homework papers as she mounted the steps. She knew that her ostrichlike mentality—hoping that if she couldn't see them, they wouldn't see her—was foolish. But she wasn't ready to face disappointment with a group of friends watching.

Suddenly Sara's books were knocked out of her hands and onto the floor as Julie's arms wrapped

around her in a gleeful hug. "We won! We won!"
Julie shouted joyously. She was hopping up and
down in excitement, her blond curls bouncing
against her shoulders and her blue eyes gleaming with delight.

Sara looked at Julie with a stunned expression. Did that mean what it seemed? Then Sara
remembered that Julie often referred to her pals
as a team; that was the "we" she meant—the
good guys won; Julie won. "Gosh, congratulations," Sara told her. "How did Mike do?"

"He won too. Can you believe it? We're all
going to be in student council together!"

Sara edged closer to the bulletin board while
Julie's attention was caught by a couple of other
students telling her how her speech had gotten
their votes. Scanning the list of homeroom teachers, Sara found Mrs. Lugano's name. Next to it
was *Sara Langdon—17; Dick Stone—14.*

She just stood there for several moments feeling the happiness wash over her. She couldn't
believe that her classmates had actually elected
her instead of Dick, but it was right there in
black and white. It wasn't a sweeping victory,
but all Sara had really expected was two votes,
Julie's and her own. To think that so many of
her classmates trusted her, an outsider, to represent them brought a lump to Sara's throat. Well,
she'd make sure they didn't regret their choice;
she'd be the best homeroom representative there
ever was.

The moment Sara and Julie entered Mrs. Lugano's room, Julie was surrounded by the rest of the homeroom. Everyone was jumping up and down and yelling and Sara realized that she was the one who was most responsible for making Julie's election a point of interest and pride for the whole class. While she stood there in an island of calm, Dick Stone walked over and held out his hand. "Congratulations," he told her. "I guess the best man for this job turned out to be a woman. I think you'll do a great job."

"Thank you," Sara said shyly. Would she have been able to be this gracious if she'd lost? she wondered.

Julie had been right about the homework. None of the teachers seemed to expect it to be done and they spent most of the time rerunning what they'd gone over the day before, indulgent smiles on their faces as kids whispered and passed congratulatory notes back and forth, paying little attention to the lecture.

Sara finally saw Mike in the hall between her math and Spanish classes. "I can see the headlines now—'L.A. girl takes charge at Overton High; locals bow to the inevitable!'" he teased. "I guess I'll have to put up with you in student council, too, now, huh?"

"Well, you could always resign if you think you really can't stand it," she said with a mischievous grin.

Mike grabbed her up in a bear hug and laughed. "Fat chance. Are we on for tonight?"

Sara realized she hadn't said anything to Uncle Ted about going to dinner with Mike. Her aunt and uncle weren't thrilled with her being out on a school night, but fortunately Aunt Liz would be back in town this afternoon. Sara felt sure she could make her aunt see that this was a special occasion. "I'll have to check," she told Mike. "But I think it'll be okay if we're not too late."

"No problem. I'll call you after practice and we'll make a plan." Mike winked at Sara and then hurried off to his next class. But as Sara turned toward Mr. Alano's room and Spanish, she caught sight of Melodie Burton watching her from across the hall. The look on Melodie's face was not one of congratulation.

Sara was a little late for lunch, and when she got there, she saw Julie sitting with Melodie and Ginger. Ginger had won the other junior senate seat and Melodie was her best friend. Scanning the room, Sara spotted Marsha and LuAnn sitting at a small table and they saw her at the same time. When they waved her over, Sara was grateful for the excuse to join them; she didn't think she could face lunch with Melodie.

Marsha had painted all of Julie's campaign posters and Sara expected her to be looking quite happy that she'd played such an important part in the victory. So she was surprised to see both girls with glum expressions on their faces.

"Don't tell Julie," Marsha said in a low voice as soon as Sara sat down. "We don't want to spoil her happy day, but we've heard some scary stuff."

Sara stared at her, wondering what she could be talking about. She was soon enlightened.

"Remember last night when I said Diane Wallace was supposed to join us but she never showed up?" Marsha went on.

Sara nodded, but before Marsha could speak, LuAnn said quickly, "We think something's happened to her."

"What do you mean?" Sara asked them.

"She's disappeared," Marsha explained. "She's in my homeroom and she wasn't there this morning, and she never made it to English class either."

Sara nodded. "I didn't see her in history second period," she said.

"I called her mom during the break between second and third periods," LuAnn broke in. "And it turns out she left the house last night about six and she never came home. Mrs. Wallace is worried sick. She called the police last night. My dad always says they can't do anything for a while because some kids just run away or something on their own. But Diane isn't the type to do something like that. Her mom's divorced and it's just the two of them, and Diane simply wouldn't do that to her mom no matter what. Besides, it's not like she had a boyfriend or something." She looked around furtively for a moment as if worried that they were being overheard. "I think she disappeared the same way Mary Jo Rice did— the ski-mask rapist must have grabbed her, and she recognized him, so he killed her."

Sara could feel the color drain from her face. She didn't want to believe what LuAnn was saying. "But no one knows for sure, right? I mean, something else could have happened."

"Like what?" Marsha sounded as if she'd given up hope.

Sara looked at LuAnn. "What does your dad say? Are they any closer to catching this guy in the ski mask?"

LuAnn shrugged. "He hasn't been talking about it lately, so maybe that's good news. I mean, if they do have a lead, he sure isn't going to tell me so I can blab it to everyone in sight," she said with a self-deprecating smile. Then her face turned grim. "All I can say is, I'd sure be careful going anywhere with anyone you don't know real well. In fact, I'd think twice about going out alone with a guy from school right now."

"From school?" Sara was horrified. "You can't believe that anyone we know could be involved in this!"

"Oh, I don't think that's really what LuAnn meant," Marsha told her quickly. "It's more that there's always safety in numbers and now it's especially important to stick with groups of kids after dark. I mean, Mary Jo's disappearing was one thing. Everybody has a theory about that. But Marlene Marrs was definitely raped by this ski-mask guy. And Diane would never go running off on her own. Something terrible must have happened."

As the three of them got up from the lunch table, Sara wondered how come it was okay for them to spoil her happy day, but she shrugged philosophically. They probably were bursting to tell somebody and she just happened to be the lucky one.

As the day wore on, Sara noticed more and more groups of girls huddled in whispered conversations. But she stayed aloof from the gossip mill and even managed to give Julie a cheery smile when she saw her. Eventually the last bell rang and Julie caught up with her as the two of them were leaving their financial-management class. "Is it true about Diane?" Julie asked as soon as they were outside on the steps.

Sara gave up the pretense; in a school this small everyone heard every rumor almost immediately and it was silly for LuAnn and Marsha to think Julie would remain ignorant for long. "I guess so," Sara replied slowly. "At least LuAnn and Marsha seemed pretty certain that something's happened to her."

"Honestly, Sara!" Julie said angrily. "You've known about this since lunch and never said a word to me! And don't pretend it isn't so—I saw you at lunch with them. The three of you were huddled together talking so hard that I figured I'd better not butt in. But if someone's kidnapped Diane or something, it affects all of us. I'm her friend too. How could you do this to me?"

"Well, LuAnn and Marsha have been your friends longer than I have, so when they asked me not to mention it to you . . ." Sara trailed off, not sure how to respond to Julie's anger.

"Right. And what if someone else hadn't told me? I mean, what if I didn't know that this rapist had struck again? I might have decided to go out for a walk by myself tonight or who knows what, and then how would you feel if this guy grabbed me and you hadn't had the decency to warn me?"

Sara looked around a little wildly for help, for someone to join them and defuse the situation. But of course no one was nearby. "Gosh, Julie, I'm sorry. I mean, you wouldn't really go out walking by yourself at night anyway, would you?"

"Of course, you wouldn't think so," Julie hissed at her. "You L.A. people never walk anywhere, do you? You probably think walking is unnatural."

Sara felt as though she'd been slapped. "At least we 'L.A. people' know something about friendship. I guess now that you're a big-deal junior senator, you don't need me or anyone else to help you get elected anymore."

"What's that supposed to mean?" Julie glared at her.

Sara glared back. "What that means is that if you had been having lunch with LuAnn and Marsha and me, you would have heard about Diane then. But you were too busy hanging out with your new best pals, Melodie and Ginger. What were you guys doing, trying to figure out how to take over the school?"

Blotches of angry color appeared on Julie's fair skin. "I don't have to stand here listening to this. You are the one who sucked up to me when you were new and didn't know anyone. How do you think you got elected as homeroom representative? If it hadn't been for me—"

Sara cut in. "What did you do, stuff the ballot box so I would win?"

Julie turned on her heel and stomped down the steps, almost running into a couple of kids who had sauntered by. Without a backward glance, she headed down the sidewalk toward her house, in the opposite direction from Sara's.

CHAPTER 7

Sara trudged home feeling forlorn and abandoned. The fight with Julie had left her devastated. Does Julie really think I was just using her to make friends here? she wondered sadly. Maybe everyone thought she was some sort of weirdo from L.A., simply taking advantage of Julie's natural friendliness.

"I'm not!" Sara said out loud as she walked along the empty sidewalk. I thought Julie and I were friends, that she actually liked me. But maybe no one at Overton really likes me, she thought. Julie's right—I wouldn't have won that election without her support. Maybe the kids who voted for me felt they had to make Julie happy.

And what about Mike? How did he really feel about her? Could Julie have engineered his interest in her too? Julie was awfully popular and had dates whenever she wanted them. She didn't seem interested in going with any one guy—

maybe Mike was really in love with Julie and thought that by being nice to Sara, he could get Julie to think more of him.

Mike was at football practice, and now with Diane's disappearance, her aunt and uncle probably wouldn't let her go out with him tonight. She wasn't even sure she wanted to.

By the time Sara got to her aunt and uncle's house, her face was stained with tear tracks. Of all the times she wanted to be alone, wouldn't you know that Aunt Liz would be back from her trip and waiting for her.

"Hi, Sara," she called from the dining room, where she was bending over dozens of scraps of fabric and wallpaper scattered all over the table.

"Hi, Aunt Liz," Sara mumbled as she yearned for the privacy of her room. But before she could even reach the stairs, her aunt trotted across the living room to intercept her.

She turned Sara toward her, and when she saw the tearstained face, put her arms around her niece's shoulders and said, "Honey, what's wrong?"

"Everything," Sara wailed through a fresh onslaught of tears.

Incorrectly guessing at the problem, her aunt said, "I heard about Diane Wallace disappearing last night—someone told me this afternoon when I stopped at the supermarket. It's really awful, isn't it? Is she a good friend of yours?"

Sara shook her head. "Not really. I mean, she hangs around with the same kids I do and I know her, but we aren't really close."

"Still, finding out that someone you actually know is in serious trouble is pretty distressing, I would imagine," Aunt Liz said gently. Sara shrugged off the comment and Aunt Liz asked, "Is there something else the matter?"

Nothing except my whole world collapsing, Sara thought, but she gave her aunt a noncommittal shake of the head.

Her aunt hugged Sara tight for a moment and then stepped back. "I know it's hard being the new kid at school, especially when you don't have your dad around either. Your uncle and I have been really pleased at how quickly you seem to have adjusted." She smiled at Sara and smoothed strands of the girl's silky dark hair away from her face. "But things don't always go along perfectly for anyone, honey. And I'm sure all the kids at school are on edge about the terrible things that have been happening. You may even be more upset about it all than you want to admit to yourself." She stroked Sara's cheek and Sara had the sudden desire to tell her aunt everything that was making her so unhappy.

But the moment passed. Sara gave a weak smile instead. "I guess I better get going on my homework."

Realizing she wouldn't hear any more, Aunt Liz said in a brisk tone, "Fine. Why don't you pick up a snack in the kitchen first, though? Dinner will be a little later than usual tonight."

By 5:30 when Mike called, Sara had spent almost two hours rereading the same pages in her American history textbook. She felt exhausted from the emotional highs and lows of the day and it was hardly a lie when she told him she didn't feel well enough to see him that night.

He sounded disappointed, and then a little angry when she continued to refuse. "It'll be a whole bunch of us going, if that's what you're worried about," he told her with a slight edge to his voice.

"I don't know what you're talking about," Sara said uncertainly.

"Oh, all the guys know the rumor that's going around—that it's one of us who's the ski-mask rapist. That one of us did something to Diane. But if you think it might be me, then I'm just trying to reassure you that you won't have to be alone with me for a minute if you don't want to be."

"Oh, Mike, that's silly," Sara said, almost crying. She wasn't up to dealing with his hurt feelings too. "I just don't want to go out tonight. I can't!"

After a moment's silence Mike finally said, "Right. Well, I guess I'll see you tomorrow. Bye."

"Goodbye," Sara whispered, but it was to the dial tone.

Tears of frustration spilled down Sara's cheeks.

First Julie and now Mike—what was she doing wrong? How had a day with such a good start ended up so miserably? And what was going to happen tomorrow? Sara lay down on her bed and pulled the comforter over herself. In minutes she was asleep.

Sara awoke about an hour later. At first she was disoriented; the sun had set and there was a rosy glow on the horizon as the autumn evening darkened. Some noise had awakened her. She cracked open the door to her room, but the voices of her aunt and uncle were coming in through her open window. They were arguing about a car. Sara straightened her clothes and washed her face before pulling a brush through her long dark hair. When she got downstairs, her aunt was setting the table in the dining room while her uncle sat in front of the television news.

With a quick hello to her uncle, Sara went in to help her aunt. A moment later Uncle Ted clicked off the TV and ambled in to join them. "I gather congratulations are in order," he said to Sara with a grin. Both Sara and Aunt Liz looked at him in amazement.

"How did you find out?" Sara stammered as Aunt Liz asked what they were talking about.

With a wink to Sara, he said to his wife, "Our little Sara has gotten herself elected to the Overton High student council. I'm surprised she didn't tell you—I heard about it this afternoon when I was picking up my new car."

"Why, Sara, that's wonderful," Aunt Liz said enthusiastically, but she gave her niece a quizzical look.

Sara shrugged. "I'm only a homeroom representative. And besides, I only won by three votes."

"Hey, kiddo, don't knock it. Winning is winning," her uncle said, giving her a hug. "I'd call that pretty terrific, especially for the new kid in town. Why don't we go to Oscar's tomorrow night for a celebration dinner? You liked that place, didn't you, Sara?"

"Sure," she said. "It was great. But tell me about your new car. I didn't know you were getting one."

Aunt Liz gave him a look and then went into the kitchen to serve the plates. After she'd left, Uncle Ted said in a low voice, "Maybe we won't talk about that too much, okay? Your aunt thinks I'm foolish to change cars so soon after I got the last one." He looked at Sara with an embarrassed boyish grin. "I got tired of dark blue—this one's green."

Sara grinned back. When Uncle Ted was in one of his charming moods, he was pretty hard to resist. Maybe that's why Aunt Liz put up with him.

At that moment Aunt Liz came through the doorway carrying two plates. "Six months ago you got tired of gray," she said with an edge to her voice.

"Come on, Liz," he said in a pleading voice as he fetched the third plate from the kitchen and then held the dining-room chair for his wife, not his usual habit. "The cars are on lease, so it's not as if it really costs us much of anything. And besides, isn't a man entitled to a little bit of fun?" Putting an end to the conversation, he turned to Sara. "Now I want to hear all about that election."

By the time dinner was over and the kitchen cleaned up, Sara was feeling much better. Maybe Aunt Liz was right and everyone at school was more tense about Diane's disappearance than they realized. She and Julie had exchanged some harsh words, but she couldn't believe that Julie had been pretending to like her all this time. What would have been the point? And she could see how Julie's feelings might have been hurt when she found out that Sara hadn't mentioned a word to her about Diane's disappearance for a whole afternoon, especially when they had been working together in the last class they shared.

Sara admitted to herself that she would have told Julie if she hadn't seen her huddled at lunch with Melodie and Ginger. Sara knew Melodie didn't like her and she felt as though Julie was taking Melodie's side. But Sara remembered that it was Julie who'd told her about Melodie and Mike and who'd warned her to watch out for Melodie.

Wishing it would all blow over by itself, and

afraid that it wouldn't and she'd lose a friend, Sara went up to her room to call Julie. At first the line was busy, but after a few more tries, Julie's mom answered the phone. She told Sara that Julie was out for the evening, but Sara thought the woman's voice sounded sort of strained. As she hung up the phone Sara wondered if Julie was really home and simply refused to talk to her. Sara pushed her hair back behind her ears and chewed on her lip in frustration. There wasn't anything she could do about it tonight. Still, she opened her schoolbooks with a heavy heart.

In the middle of the night the carnival began in Sara's mind again. She was back in the house of mirrors and the raucous music was almost deafening. She caught the reflection of the man in the ski mask behind her, but when she turned around, he was gone. Colored lights strobed up from the floor and down from the ceiling, surrounding Sara in a whirl of confusion.

She heard screams off to one direction and fought her way through the maze to follow them. "Help me!" a girl's voice called, but when Sara tried to call back that she was on her way, she couldn't. No matter how hard she tried, whenever she opened her mouth to scream, no sound came out.

The mirrors were really flexible sheets of reflective material that seemed to hang on chains from the ceiling. Sara pushed at the one in front of her and it swung out of her way only to reveal another a few feet away. Every direction she turned she was caught in the maze of sound and light.

Then suddenly everything was dark and still. It was as if someone had pulled the plug on a sound-and-light machine. She put her hands out in front of her, trying to feel her way. But her hands touched nothing except air—the mirrors were gone. Under her feet the concrete floor had become bumpy and soft. She tried to call out again, and this time her voice came back to her, echoing over and over. She took another cautious step forward, straining to hear any sound beside her own rapid breathing. As she put her foot down the ground under her gave way and she was falling through a black void.

Sara flailed out, trying to stop her tumbling fall. I'm moving so fast, I'll be squished like a bug on the sidewalk when I land, she thought desperately.

Sara's eyes flew open and slowly the familiar shapes of her room at Aunt Liz and Uncle Ted's came into focus. Her twisting and turning had tangled the sheets around her, and as she pulled herself free of the covers, she realized that she was soaked in perspiration. She lay still for a few minutes, waiting for her thumping heart to calm while reassuring herself that she was safe at home.

The glowing numbers on her alarm clock read 3:11. Unwilling to face the glare of her bedside lamp, Sara got out of bed in the dark and crept into the bathroom for a glass of water. By the time she crawled under the covers, she was almost asleep again.

This time she found herself back at the carnival riding a horse on the carousel. Her stallion was big and brawny with a sleek black coat and snorting nostrils. It pranced up and down and threw its head about wildly. Sara hung on with all her might, but the pole going down through the animal's neck and body kept slipping in her hands and she was afraid she was going to be thrown off.

It was the most peculiar carousel Sara had ever been on. She rode in the outside circle of horses, next to the edge of the platform. The next circle in consisted of painted and saddled rabbits and dogs and cats leaping and hopping in place, but that circle moved faster than Sara's did. A prissy poodle moved past her horse and then a wimpy-looking rabbit. Sara turned her head and looked over her shoulder to see what was approaching next. A big snarling dog leaped into view, and on its back was the man in the ski mask.

He held tight to his pole with one hand while he reached out the other trying to grab Sara. She screamed and shouted at him to leave her alone, but the jolly calliope music drowned out her words. Sara leaned away from the man and his dog whizzed by without him touching her.

A few seconds later he was back again, reaching out his long arm to snag at her flying hair. Sara leaned farther over the outside of her horse, using the animal as a shield between herself and the man in the ski mask.

He'll catch me the next time, she thought as she clung to the side of her horse while the man in the ski mask loped past her on his still-snarling dog. If only I could get off. But her horse's feet were right next to the edge of the platform. There was no room for her to dismount on that side, and climbing down from the other side would put her within the man's grasp. The merry-go-round sped up and suddenly Sara's horse broke loose from its pole and raced off through the carnival grounds. It jumped over an ice-cream cart and zigzagged between concession stands. Sara clung to the animal's mane and flung a terrified look over her shoulder. The man on the dog had left the carousel too and was running after her. His ski mask was gone, but she couldn't see his face.

Sara urged her horse on, but the man was gaining on them. He was closing in on her left and all Sara could do was lean far to the right over the side of her horse. The man's hand reached out again and Sara screamed in terror. He was coming closer and closer. . . .

Thump. Sara rolled off her bed and landed on the carpeted floor. Gray morning light came in through the open window and her clock read a few minutes after six. Wearily Sara got up. The room was cold and she pulled on her fleecy robe. There was no way she was going back to bed at this point. She might as well get showered and dressed.

As Sara flipped on the bathroom heat lamp and then stood under the hot, pulsing shower she couldn't shake the frightening images of the dream from her mind.

CHAPTER 8

Having gotten up so early that morning, Sara decided she might as well use the extra time to good advantage. Besides, nothing she'd studied the afternoon and evening before had stuck in her brain. So she went into the school library and spread her books and papers all over one of the tables.

There was no one there except the school librarian, Mrs. Tipper, who always had the library open by seven. She smiled hello and after Sara had settled herself came over and said, "I'm just going to run into the teachers' lounge for a cup of coffee. You won't need anything from me for a while, will you?"

Sara shook her head. "Thanks, but I'm just here to catch up on some studying."

Mrs. Tipper patted Sara's shoulder. "Good for you. I wish more students would take advantage of the library. It's so nice and quiet, tucked away like it is. None of the school noise will disturb you here. Well, I'll be back shortly. But you mustn't wait for me if you need to leave, just make sure the door is unlocked. The students here are quite trustworthy and we've rarely lost a book."

As Sara watched the older woman totter out on her impossibly high heels, she realized that she'd never heard Mrs. Tipper say more than three words before. Of course, Sara thought, she might not get much opportunity. Most of the kids just stopped by to check out the books they needed and left. Sara had assumed from the few times she'd seen Mrs. Tipper that the woman wasn't much of a conversationalist, but maybe she was dying for company and rarely had anyone to talk to.

The library was certainly lonely. Even though Sara knew that by now there must be students banging locker doors open and shut and calling to one another in the halls, no sound came through the partially open library door. The long narrow room had been added onto the main school building at some point in the distant past. There were several of these odd-shaped additions sticking out from the sides and back of the original square brick building. And, of course, book-lined walls and a carpeted floor would probably muffle sounds pretty effectively.

Sara's eyes returned to her textbook, and she was so deeply engrossed in what she was reading that she didn't hear the soft click of the door closing a few minutes later. With a start she heard the voice of the person who'd come in. "My, my, and what have we here? Ms. Hollywood studying? I thought you already knew it all."

It was Rick Black. Sara sighed under her breath. No matter what she said, he twisted it to make her sound as though she was a stuck-up snot from the big city. Unfortunately today Diane Wallace wasn't there to put him in his place.

Now he towered over the table where she sat. "What's the matter, cat got your tongue? Or are you just trying to decide which of your devastating put-downs will be most effective?"

Sara almost bit her tongue keeping back exactly the kind of retort he'd described. Give it a rest, she thought. Then, smiling sweetly, she said, "Mrs. Tipper asked me to tell anyone who came in that she'd be back in a bit."

Rick sneered at Sara. "She did, did she?" His voice was soft and menacing as he sidled around the table toward her. "Well, I guess that means we're all alone in here for a while. Just you and me, Sara."

He'd moved up next to her chair and was reaching out his hand for her when Sara panicked. Grabbing up one of the heavy volumes sitting in front of her on the table, she swung it as hard as she could into his gut. Before Rick could recover from the blow, Sara shoved back her chair, snatched up her purse, and ran for the library door.

The hallway between the library and the main building was deserted. With a quick glance over her shoulder Sara raced toward the lively sounds of students only a few yards away.

As she entered the main hall Sara slowed down, taking comfort from the normalcy that now surrounded her. Students were stuffing jackets and sweaters in their lockers while at the same time trying to juggle armloads of books. A couple of girls nearby were practicing Spanish-verb conjugations with each other, boning up for a test. One of the sophomore boys was nonchalantly leaning against the wall talking to his girlfriend. Sara recognized his posture as an exact duplication of the way Mike stood against the wall when he was talking to her. A bunch of guys were boasting about their tryouts for the junior varsity, trying to attract the attention of the girls practicing their Spanish.

Even though Sara's locker wasn't in this part of the school, she recognized some of the kids. They were mostly a year younger than she, and while a few smiled hello, they paid little attention to her as she walked briskly by.

Sara glanced over her shoulder a few times. Once she caught sight of Mrs. Tipper daintily clicking along in her high heels from the other end of the hall toward the corridor to the library. But there was no sign of Rick behind her. She was tempted to go back to the library now that Mrs. Tipper was there. Her notebook and a couple of textbooks still sat on that library table and Sara needed them for class. Then she shook her head. No, she'd make a detour on her way from homeroom to English; he'd certainly be gone by then. She didn't want to take the chance that she'd run into Rick again.

What was the matter with him anyway? Now that her breathing had subsided to a normal rate and her heart was no longer thumping in her throat, Sara reconsidered what had happened. Rick hadn't exactly threatened her. In fact, what he had said would probably come across as harmless joking to anyone who hadn't been there. But Sara had been there, and she had been scared.

She knew Rick didn't like her, but there was a big difference between not liking someone and wanting to hurt her. Unbidden, the thought sprang into Sara's mind. What if Rick was the rapist who had been terrorizing the school? After all, rape wasn't something a guy did to someone he liked. It was an act of hostile violence. And Rick certainly was hostile, at least to her.

The buzzer sounded, and as Sara hurried along to homeroom she decided to find out what Rick had been doing the night before last when Diane Wallace disappeared. It was hard to believe that someone she knew, even someone she didn't like, could do anything that horrible. But now that the idea had taken hold of her mind, Sara knew she'd have to follow it through until she found out, one way or the other.

It wasn't until she'd slid into her seat and looked around for Julie that Sara remembered the fight they'd had the afternoon before. She had been so upset about the confrontation with Rick that she'd totally forgotten that she and Julie might not be friends anymore. But Julie wasn't there.

Sara was beginning to wonder if something was wrong when Julie raced into the room just as tardy bell rang. Mrs. Lugano looked up in disapproval, but her expression changed to an understanding smile when she saw which student had zoomed in at the last moment. Probably Julie had been out in the hall, absorbed in congratulations from her friends. Not that Mrs. Lugano approved of students being late, but she felt she could make an exception in this case.

However, Sara wasn't so sure that Julie's late entrance was a mistake. Maybe her friend had been ducking her, stalling her arrival in the room until there wasn't a chance for the two of them to talk. Julie continued to direct her attention to Mrs. Lugano at the front of the room, and Sara's heart sank. How could she patch up an argument when she didn't even really know what it was about? And it didn't look as though Julie was planning to make it any easier.

When homeroom ended, Julie was out the door before Sara could get up her nerve to say something. Sara looked around for her in the hall, but Julie was nowhere to be seen, so Sara sadly trudged down to the library to find her stuff neatly stacked on one corner of the table she'd been using. As she headed for Mr. Wright's room Sara wondered if Julie was going to avoid her all day.

The seating plan for English class meant that Sara and Julie sat at opposite corners of the room, with Julie up front near the door and Sara in the back by the windows. Sara scanned the hall in vain, looking for her friend and then finally went in and sat down. Once again, Julie scooted into her seat at the last moment. As the class came to a close Sara packed up her stuff; she wanted to be ready to leave the minute the bell rang. She wasn't going to have Julie disappear on her again.

But when Sara got into the hall, she saw Melodie and Ginger come out of the classroom opposite and start talking to Julie. Melodie caught sight of Sara and gave her a look and then turned her attention back to the other two girls. That snub was the last straw, and Sara turned on her heel and marched off. If that's the way Julie wants to be, then let her, she thought.

As Sara neared her next class, American history, her steps slowed. What she really didn't need was another confrontation with Rick. She was already feeling nervous about running into him when she felt a large male hand on her shoulder. Whirling around, she was relieved to see Jeff, one of Mike's best friends. "Hey, what happened to you last night?" he asked. "Mike was kind of bummed out when you couldn't make it."

Maybe Mike really does like me, Sara thought, her heart lightening. She improvised quickly. "Well, I don't know what was the matter—I thought I was getting the flu. But I'm fine today. Did you guys have fun?"

Jeff grinned. "We always have fun. Anyway, I'm glad you're okay now. I'll tell Mike. I think he was kind of worried about you."

At that moment Melodie strolled by. "Hi, Jeff," she said, pretending that she didn't see Sara.

The smile dropped from Jeff's face. "Hi, Mel," he said coolly. Then he grinned at Sara again. "Catch ya later—I've got to run."

As Sara entered Mr. Merritt's class she caught sight of Rick across the room. He was talking with a couple of his pals, and when he saw Sara, he nudged one of the other guys. Her self-confidence much improved after her conversation with Jeff, Sara decided once again that the best way to deal with Rick was to ignore him totally. Still, it wasn't easy to walk across the room to her desk. Rick had planted himself up front near the windows not far from where Sara sat.

Sara spotted LuAnn at her desk near the rear of the room. She walked back to talk to her and hoped that she could outwait Rick and his friends; the buzzer telling them all to sit down should ring any second. Out of the corner of her eye Sara saw Rick moving her way. Surely he wouldn't do anything truly scary with thirty other kids right there. She was so focused on Rick's approach that she never heard a word LuAnn was saying.

Then the bell rang and Mr. Merritt was calling the class to order; Sara ran up the far aisle and slid into her seat. She could feel Rick's eyes on her as she kept her own face turned toward the front of the room. It was as if he was waiting for something, and a few minutes later she knew what it was. Her American-history textbook was one of the ones she'd left in the library. When she opened it to the chapter they were studying, a half sheet of notebook paper was stuck between the pages. *You could be next* was scrawled across the piece of paper.

Sara felt the color rise up her neck and into her cheeks. She was positive Rick had put the note in her book. He'd no doubt done it after she'd run out of the library that morning. But what did it mean? Why couldn't he just leave her alone? If he was really the rapist, would he be so stupid as to advertise the fact that he was after her? Sara's first instinct was to crumple the paper and toss it in the trash, but on second thought she decided to leave it where it was. She didn't want to give Rick the satisfaction of knowing that he'd gotten to her, and besides, if he turned out to be the rapist, the police might want the note. The rest of the class period Sara was lost in thought about how she could find out what Rick was doing on Monday night.

CHAPTER 9

Just before lunch Sara stopped at her locker to drop off her books and found Mike there waiting for her. He was leaning nonchalantly against the wall, and she was reminded of the sophomore boy's identical stance earlier in the day. Did the younger guys imitate all the postures of the senior big shots, she wondered? She smiled to herself. She'd have to remember to watch for copycat gestures and see.

Assuming that Sara's smile was for him, Mike reached out, grabbing her books with one large hand and giving her a hug with the other arm. "Missed you last night," he said.

"I know," Sara said with a grin. "I saw Jeff and he told me. You'd better be careful of pals who give you away like that. Pretty soon I'll know all your secrets!"

Mike laughed. "Not a chance. I don't even tell myself some of my secrets." He loaded Sara's books onto the top shelf of her locker. "Did you see the notice about the first student council meeting? It's tomorrow after school."

Sara shook her head and Mike went on. "I guess nobody told you that they put a notice on the bulletin board out by the main entrance a day or two before. But don't worry, they'll announce it during homeroom tomorrow morning."

Great, Sara thought with a sigh, now I won't be able to go in and talk to Ms. Simon about the chemistry test on Friday—I'll just have to hope I know the stuff.

Mike noticed her unhappy expression. "Hey, don't worry about it. I was homeroom rep on council last year and it's a piece of cake. You got any questions about it, just ask me."

Suddenly Sara was reminded about Rick. "Actually I do have a question for you, but not about student council. Remember on Monday night after the election you went out with a bunch of the guys?" Mike got a funny look on his face, but Sara went on. "Was Rick Black along that night?"

Mike continued to look uncomfortable. He looked down at his feet as he spoke. "Well, I don't really know. I mean, I didn't exactly go out with the guys like we'd planned."

"You didn't?" Sara asked, surprised. "How come?"

Mike looked nervously around the hall. "Oh, something else came up is all. Oh, there's Jeff.

Gotta run. Catch ya later."

Wow, that was strange, Sara thought as Mike joined his buddy and headed toward the cafeteria. She knew that Mike and Jeff and a bunch of the other guys from the team always ate lunch together, but why did he seem so eager to leave all of a sudden? She shrugged her shoulders. Sometimes guys were so weird. Anyway, the important thing was that she still didn't know where Rick was that night, and now she didn't have a clue how to find out.

When Sara walked into the cafeteria, it was like déjà vu from yesterday. There were Julie and Melodie and Ginger huddled together at one small table, and a bunch of the other girls at another, bigger one. What's with you, Julie? Sara said to herself.

It wasn't as if Julie and Melodie and Ginger had been such close buddies before the election. Melodie and Ginger were best friends and together all the time, but Julie generally hung out with a larger crowd. And until yesterday she and I were best friends, Sara thought bitterly. Then she grabbed a tray of food and slowly made her way to the big table where LuAnn and Marsha and a bunch of the other girls were sitting.

Sara pulled out a chair on the far side of the table so her back would be to Julie. Don't be such a baby, she scolded herself as she made an effort to tune in to the conversation in progress around her. Be grateful you've got any group of friends to sit with. You're only going to be here for one year, so make the most of it. But in her mind Sara saw the months ahead without Julie's friendship stretching out into a dismal infinity.

With her back to the room, Sara couldn't tell when Julie left the cafeteria and she didn't see her in the halls between classes. But they shared their last-period class and Sara was determined to make another stab at putting their friendship back together.

Sara changed her clothes after gym in record time. She wanted to get to her Hands-On Econ class as early as possible and try to waylay Julie on her way into the room. When she got there, Ms. Brooks was madly scribbling numbers on the board. "Oh, hi, Sara," Ms. Brooks said. "Do me a favor and put one of these packets of papers on each desk, will you please?"

Sara had no choice but to grab up the huge stack of stapled-together papers from the teacher's desk and start distributing them. She started at the end of the room farthest from Julie's desk, figuring that she could finish before the bell rang and wait for Julie there. But once again Julie was almost tardy for class, and by the time she was sliding into her seat, Ms. Brooks was saying, "Please sit down, everyone, and let's get started. We have a lot to cover this period."

In spite of her worries, Sara found herself quickly caught up in Ms. Brooks's explanation of how mutual funds work. Almost before she knew it, the bell had rung and school was over for the day. Julie practically flew out the door, so Sara grabbed up her books and ran out into the hall after her. "Julie, wait!" she called, but the other girl had sped around the corner. She has to go to her locker before she leaves the building, Sara decided, heading that way.

After half an hour of waiting near Julie's locker, Sara realized she might as well give up. The halls were empty and the only kids still left at school were the guys out on the football field practicing. She couldn't imagine how Julie had been to her locker and left school so fast, but that's what must have happened. As Sara trudged wearily to her own locker she wondered if she was trying to fight fate. After all, Julie had made it pretty clear that she didn't even want to talk to her again. So why are you trying to track her down and work things out? Sara asked herself. Do you need her to tell you in words of one syllable that she wants you out of her life before you give up?

Maybe it was the muleheaded stubbornness that her dad was always kidding her about, or maybe it was because she really did care for Julie and wasn't willing to let the friendship go without giving it every possible chance. Whatever was urging her on, Sara knew she was going to walk over to Julie's house and camp out on her doorstep all night if necessary. One way or the other she was going to talk to Julie.

Julie's house was in the other direction from school, and as Sara walked through the drifts of fall leaves, she thought about how far it was going to be if she ended up having to walk all the way home. What if Julie was so mad at her that she wouldn't even let her in to call Aunt Liz to come and pick her up?

A chilly wind brought more leaves down from the trees, and Sara had another unhappy thought. Suppose no one was home at Julie's house? It would be getting dark before too long, and the sweater Sara had worn to school wouldn't be much help in keeping her warm if she was standing around on Julie's front step. It was barely warm enough while she was walking.

As Sara crossed the street to Julie's block she tried to rehearse what she might say. But nothing came to mind. Maybe this was a truly dumb idea. After all, she'd see Julie in school tomorrow and the girl couldn't stay away from her forever.

When she got to Julie's house, Sara's fears all seemed to be coming true at once. The wind had gotten stronger, pushing heavy gray clouds across the sky. The air smelled like rain. Julie's house looked empty and forlorn, and there was no car in the driveway. Suspecting it was hopeless, she walked up to the front door and rang the bell. She could hear it doing its musical-chime number inside the house, but there were no answering footsteps coming toward the door. Sara tried the bell again, but the house was empty.

Sara stepped back from the door and looked around, wondering what to do next. It had been one thing to make a vow to wait at Julie's when Sara was inside the warm, brightly lit school building and not far from home. But now she was miles from Aunt Liz and Uncle Ted's, and to add to her misery, the first drops of rain splashed on her nose and chin. She moved closer to Julie's front door, knowing that the tiny overhang would be little protection from the sudden storm that seemed to have come out of nowhere. The wind howled around her, and soon the pelting rain was soaking through to her skin.

Just as she had decided to run to a neighbor's house and see if someone would let her use the phone, Julie's mom's car swung around the corner. Thank heaven, Sara thought. At least Julie's mom can't be mad at me. She'll let me in to call Aunt Liz; maybe she'll even drive me home herself.

But the person behind the wheel was Julie. She looked upset when she got out and slammed the door behind her. "What are you doing here?" she yelled at Sara as she stood next to the car in the pouring rain.

Oh, Julie, don't be so mad at me you won't even let me in, prayed Sara. "I walked over from school. I wanted to talk to you," she yelled back.

Julie muttered something under her breath and then called, "I don't have a key to the front door. Hang on a second." With that she splashed through the flood between the driveway and side door and disappeared inside.

To Sara it seemed like an eternity, but actually less than two minutes later Julie was unbolting the front door. She pushed open the storm door and dragged Sara inside. "Are you crazy or what?" Julie said in a cross tone. "You look like a drowned rat. Don't move."

Sara stood there sodden and dripping as she watched Julie pad across the living room in her soggy sock feet. A moment later Julie was back with a stack of towels. "Here," she said, thrusting the towels at Sara. "Dry yourself off before you catch pneumonia. You'd probably better take your clothes off too. I'll put them in the dryer."

With that Julie was off again, running up the stairs to her room. While she was gone Sara stripped off her clothes and left them in a wet pile in the puddle she'd formed on the floor. She wrapped one of the big bath sheets around her, but a moment later Julie returned carrying a long fleecy robe.

As Julie tried to hand it over, Sara protested, "I can't wear that. It's your best robe. You love that robe—you said you'd never ever loan it to anyone."

Julie draped the robe around Sara's shoulders. "Don't be silly, Sara. You're not just anyone—you're my best friend."

Sara's mouth dropped open in surprise. "But we had a fight. . . ."

"Oh, that," Julie said dismissively. "I guess you didn't know what a hothead I am sometimes. Anyway, I was going to apologize to you, but—"

"I was trying to apologize to you," Sara broke in, "but you wouldn't even talk to me. You were like the invisible person at school—zipping into every class just as the tardy bell rang and grabbing your books and taking off the moment class was over. I waited for you at your locker after school today, but you never showed up. So I came over here to try to talk to you because I was so upset you were mad at me."

Sara was crying by the time she finished her story and she could see that Julie's eyes were filled with tears too. "Oh, you goof," Julie said, giving her a hug. "I'd never get that mad at you."

"Then why were you ignoring me?"

Julie began picking up Sara's wet clothes, and then the two of them went through to the laundry room as Julie explained. "Well, first of all, I wasn't ignoring you exactly. Mostly I was upset because of my dad."

"Your dad?"

"Yeah, he's in the hospital."

"Oh, no," Sara said softly. "What's the matter with him?" Flashes of her own mother's illness and death came flooding back to her. Even though she had been pretty young at the time, she could remember how scared she was. And the image of her father's preoccupation, the way he'd run off to the hospital every chance he got, was a vivid picture in her mind.

"Well, he's okay now, I guess. At first they thought he'd had a heart attack." Julie's voice held the remnants of fear. "He kind of passed out at work and they took him to the hospital. But they've given him every test there is, and it looks like it was just stress."

"Wow. You must have been terrified."

Julie grinned through the tears on her cheeks. "Yeah, I guess I was a little. Anyway, all I could think about at school was him. I called my mom between classes to find out what was happening, and I couldn't wait to get home and go over to the hospital to see him. That's where I just was. My mom's still there and one of her friends is going to drive her home later."

Sara hugged her friend and then used one of the towels to dry Julie's face. "I'm so sorry," she said. "I wish you'd told me. At least you would have had someone to talk to about it. It's horrible to go through that by yourself." As she looked at her friend's face Sara flashed on the lunches Julie had had with Melodie and Ginger. Julie must have told them.

But she kept the thought to herself as Julie shook her head. "I just couldn't talk about it. I guess I was afraid saying the words out loud would make it too real. Anyway, it looks like it's all okay now. The doctor said that Dad could come home tomorrow after they give him a diet and a bunch of exercises he's supposed to do." Julie grinned. "He's really going to hate that, but my mom's happy that someone is finally making him listen to reason."

Her questions about Julie's discussions with Melodie and Ginger kept crowding into Sara's mind, but she didn't think now was the time to bring them up. She was just grateful that Mr. Baker was getting out of the hospital with nothing worse than a diet-and-exercise plan. Still, Sara felt an underlying tension that she couldn't explain.

"Come on," Julie said. "There's some hot-chocolate mix and microwave popcorn in the kitchen. And this looks like the perfect day for them." Rain was pounding against the windows and the two girls could see flashes of lightning in the darkening sky.

"Sounds like a good idea to me," Sara responded. "And maybe I'd better call Aunt Liz and let her know where I am."

As Sara picked up the phone in the kitchen, Julie suggested, "Why don't you stay here for dinner?"

"Microwave popcorn and hot chocolate?"

Sara asked with a laugh.

Julie laughed too. "Maybe we can scrounge up something a little more nutritious."

By the time Sara had made her phone call, the popcorn and cocoa were ready. The two of them trailed into the living room and settled down on the couch. The drapes of the big picture window were open, and as Julie went to close them Sara said, "Oh, don't. Can't we leave the lights off and look out? I never get to see a real thunderstorm in L.A. It's really neat, sort of like Halloween. I feel like we should be telling ghost stories or something."

They sat there for a few minutes watching lightning streak across the sky and waiting for the thunderclaps to follow. Wind tore at the trees, and somewhere at the back of the house a branch banged against one of the windows. Finally Julie said, "Look, Sara, there's something I've got to tell you."

Oh, no, Sara thought. Here it comes. She really is mad at me about something and all this friendliness has only been acting. Sara had suspected there was more to Julie's strange behavior the last two days than her dad's illness. She waited and finally Julie went on. "I was hoping I could solve it all by myself and not let on to you; I didn't want your feelings to be hurt."

Sara was practically screaming with frustration. Get on with it, Julie, she almost said out loud. Instead she said lightly, "I'm not some china doll, Julie. I can handle bad news."

"Well," Julie began slowly, "it's about the election." Then it all came out in a rush. "Remember that crack you made about my stuffing the ballot box for you in homeroom? Well, a friend of Melodie's overheard it and told Mel and Ginger. Mel's not on student council, but Ginger is, and she'll do anything Mel tells her. And you know that Mel is already pissed at you about Mike— I thought she was just a little bent out of shape, but she's really crazed on the subject. So she's decided that there's no way you could have possibly won that election fairly because you're so new. I don't know whether she thinks that we somehow forced people to vote for you or if she actually thinks we rigged the election. But whatever, she wants you booted off student council. And Ginger is going to bring it up at tomorrow's meeting."

"But that's insane," Sara said. "Who would believe something like that?"

Julie sighed. "That's just the problem." She looked at Sara sadly. "You *are* new here. And there are some kids who think you're stuck-up because you're from L.A." Sara started to protest, but Julie continued. "I know it's not fair, most of those kids don't even know you. But a few people besides Melodie are already unhappy that you've snatched up the star of the football team for yourself and now you've got one of the seats on the student council." She took a breath. Saying this was even harder than she'd thought it'd be. "You're only going to be at Overton one year. Most of the kids at school have spent their whole lives here. It's not so hard to understand how some of them might feel that you've just whipped in here and skimmed off the cream to enjoy for a year. And then you'll be back in L.A."

Sara felt like she was going to throw up. She didn't want to take anything away from anyone; she just wanted to go to school and be like the other kids. The way Julie put it, she sounded like a monster. Sick at heart, she let her eyes meet Julie's. "Is that what you think too?" she asked.

"Oh, Sara, of course not," Julie said, throwing her arms around her friend in a hug. "It's just that I want you to understand that Mel and Ginger's threat is serious. I've tried and tried to talk them out of going through with this, but they're really determined."

A big load lifted from Sara's heart. "So that's what you were doing huddled with them at lunch?"

"Sure, not that it did much good." Julie looked searchingly at Sara. "It's really awful that some people can be so small-minded and mean. I didn't want you to get hurt, Sara. And I thought I could stop this whole thing before it got started, but I can't. Now I'm afraid that tomorrow's meeting is going to be really ugly," she concluded sadly.

"You know," Sara said slowly, "this won't stop with my seat on the student council. Melodie and kids like her won't be satisfied if I resign. Pretty soon they'll be pressuring Mike to stop seeing me. They'll make it harder and harder for you to keep being my friend. They'll try to freeze me out totally until no one will have anything to do with me."

Julie looked at her in horror. "Do you really think that's what she wants?"

"Maybe not right now. But bullies like her don't quit when someone backs away. They need to keep pushing and pushing."

"Oh, Sara, I'm sorry I ever got you involved in all this. If I hadn't nominated you for student council, maybe Melodie would have left you alone," Julie wailed.

From somewhere inside her came strength that Sara never knew she had. "That's not so. Melodie would have found something else. But at least this isn't going to be the sneak attack she wants it to be. I may not be a member of student council for long, but while I am, I'm not going to just roll over and play dead for her."

"What can we do?" Julie asked.

"I don't know," Sara admitted. "But maybe we can think up a plan."

CHAPTER 10

In spite of the fact that they'd polished off an entire bag of popcorn and several cups of cocoa, by 6:30 both Sara and Julie felt as though they hadn't eaten for days. And they still hadn't resolved the problem of what to do about the student council meeting tomorrow.

Julie called her mom at the hospital and found out that Mrs. Baker was having dinner with her husband in his room. "Why don't we go over to Jake's and have pizza?" Julie suggested. "It's hardly raining at all and the storm will probably blow over completely by the time we get there."

"Sounds good to me," Sara replied. "I'm starving. It must be all this thinking. Is pizza good food for the brain?"

Julie laughed. "Definitely. I'm sure I read that somewhere."

On the way to Jake's Julie said, "You know Mike is going to be really mad when he hears about this. Maybe if he told Melodie off—"

"No way," Sara said, interrupting her. "That would only make things worse. Besides, I'm not some delicate flower who needs a big man to come and defend me. We can figure out something ourselves."

Jake's usually had a light crowd on school nights and the storm seemed to have scared off even the regulars. Julie and Sara had the place almost to themselves. They settled into the back booth; the high booth backs gave them a feeling of total privacy, although there was no one nearby to hear them anyway. As they each slid second slices from the pizza pan onto their plates, a group of guys from school came in. One of them was Rick Black.

"Uh-oh," Sara said, slumping down farther in her seat and trying to become invisible.

Julie's back was to the door. She peered around the edge of the booth and then turned back to Sara. "What's the problem?"

"Look, Julie, I don't want to sound paranoid or anything, but don't you think Rick is a little weird?"

Julie laughed. "Oh, he's kind of a smart aleck sometimes. I'm always telling him his mouth is going to get him into trouble yet."

"But you don't think he's violent, or dangerous, or anything like that?" Sara persisted.

"Well, he's got kind of a temper," Julie said in an offhand way. "But if you want to see a

short fuse, just wait until you catch Mike sometime when he gets steamed about something."
She laughed at her friend's look of astonishment.
"You'd never think a sweetheart like Mike could
get violent, but believe me, when he blows up,
watch out."

Sara was pleased to see that Rick and his
pals had ordered takeout. A few moments later
they'd picked up their pizzas and left. She was
glad that he hadn't noticed her, but she certainly
wasn't making any headway in finding out if he
was really the rapist. Maybe she'd blown that
incident in the library all out of proportion. Still,
she couldn't ignore the way her gut tightened
whenever he was around.

As Sara reached for her third slice of pizza
her thoughts returned to the problem with the
student council. "I really don't know what to do
about Ginger and Melodie," she told Julie. "Of
course if I keep eating like this, I'll turn into a
blimp and then I can just sit on both of them.
They'll never be able to move."

Julie speculatively eyed Sara's slender form
and then reached for another slice herself.
"You've got an awfully long way to go, if that's
your plan. While I, on the other hand . . ." She
bit into the oozing combination of toppings and
the two of them burst into laughter.

After a moment Sara said more seriously, "The
only thing I can think of is to meet them head-
on."

"What do you mean?" Julie asked.

Sara paused, trying to corral the random thoughts that were refusing to gel in her brain. Finally she said, "What if I suggested a re-vote? Maybe I could say that I know some people are wondering how a new girl in school could get elected and I'm worried that I won't be able to represent my homeroom well if the other kids on the council can't take me seriously."

"That's great!" Julie exclaimed. "It makes you sound like a right-minded person—"

"I am a right-minded person," Sara said indignantly.

"Well, you know what I mean. Anyway, everyone would know that you care and then it would all be okay."

Sara shook her head. "No, we'd really have to have another vote."

"But, Sara, what if you lose?" Julie was dismayed.

"I probably will," Sara said with a sigh. "But my reputation at school is more important than a seat on the student council. And besides, I really couldn't do a good job knowing that some of the kids think I stole the election somehow. This way at least they'll see that I care more about the school and the student government than about myself. And maybe a few of the ones who think I'm stuck-up will change their minds."

Julie had barely been listening to Sara. Instead her mind was coming up with ways to help her friend win another homeroom election. "I must have some clout with those kids in homeroom," she said almost to herself. "Now, would it be better if I gave a little speech promoting Sara or if I just talked to people individually?"

"Don't do either one." Sara's voice was firm. "You've got to promise me that you won't do any campaigning for me." She saw Julie about to protest and held up her hand. "I mean it, Julie. That would totally destroy any credibility I have. The only way to do this is to have the election be a surprise to the homeroom on Friday morning. If we go around talking about it, then we'll be doing almost what I've been accused of. It wouldn't be fair."

Julie looked outraged. "Fair to whom? Everybody gets to campaign for elections. This way you're just guaranteeing that you'll lose."

"Well, that wouldn't be so bad. I mean, I'd be sorry not to be on the council. I think we could do a lot of neat things for the school if we all worked together. But Dick Stone is okay and he'll do a fine job." Sara felt her heart constrict as she said the words. She wanted more than anything to be on student council. She could still feel her secret elation when she'd found out she'd won. But she could never let Julie know how much it meant to her. If Julie knew how much she cared, there would be no way to stop her from doing something about it.

By the time she dropped Sara off at Aunt Liz's

house, Julie was convinced that her friend's plan was totally nuts. But once Sara made up her mind, it seemed impossible to change it. So Julie promised faithfully not to breathe a word to anyone.

The next day at school Sara found herself looking at the kids around her with a new perspective.

CHAPTER 11

No one else in their homeroom seemed to notice anything, but Sara was on pins and needles the whole period, worrying that Julie would start campaigning for her. Once she caught Julie making some comment about how lucky they all were to have such a dedicated homeroom representative on student council, and it was all Sara could do to keep herself from leaping across the aisle and throttling her. But one very stern look from Sara quelled Julie's vocal enthusiasm.

The rest of the morning bumped along pretty much as usual. Sara had hoped to find out more of Rick's whereabouts on election night when Diane Wallace disappeared. She thought there might be some way she could bring the subject up with Rick during the American-history class they shared. But it was hard finding out about someone who barely spoke to you, and eventually Sara gave up. Trying to talk to Rick was pointless. She'd just have to figure out another way to find out what he was up to.

At lunch Melodie and Ginger shared a table for two and kept their eyes on Julie and Sara. Acting according to Sara's plan, she and Julie sat at the same large table but at opposite ends so that they couldn't possibly be telling each other secrets. Sara wanted Melodie and Ginger to be surprised by her move for a revote and hoped that if she and Julie didn't appear to be very friendly, the other two girls wouldn't suspect that Julie had already told Sara of their plans. Even if Melodie and Ginger realized that Julie had shared their plan with her, Sara hoped there would be no way they could figure out her next move.

Julie and Sara didn't even go through the lunch line together, and by the time Sara had settled into her seat at the table, she realized that Diane Wallace's disappearance was again the topic of conversation.

"Are you sure it was really Diane?" Marsha asked LuAnn earnestly.

LuAnn glared across the table at Marsha and then shook her head in disbelief. "Of course I'm sure. It was her own mom. Do you think *she* made a mistake?"

Marsha's eyes dropped to her plate, where she was shoving her food from one side to the other but not eating any of it. "No," she said slowly. "But it's so hard to imagine. I mean, she was hanging out with the rest of us just a week ago."

"Someone's seen Diane?" Sara broke in excitedly. "That's really great. So she's okay?"

Sara found eight pairs of eyes staring at her. Obviously she'd missed an important piece of information. "They found her body, Sara." Julie's voice was sad.

"Oh, no," Sara cried. She looked at the other girls at the table. It couldn't be true—it must be a mistake. But it wasn't. The circle of grim faces told her that a girl they all knew—someone their own age, in their own class at school—had been killed. Sara looked at LuAnn, who seemed to know more than the rest of them. "Where was she? Do they have any clues?"

Patiently LuAnn explained what she'd obviously already told the others. "Her body was in the river. A couple of men found her last night. But my dad says that isn't where she died. She was strangled and it happened somewhere else."

Sara sank back in her chair and gazed blankly at LuAnn's serious face. It couldn't be real—it was like one of those TV movies where you knew the blood was just makeup. But it's real, another part of her mind told her. Diane—that nice, quiet girl who was Marsha's good friend. Sara remembered how Diane had stood up to Rick when he'd been tormenting her. Actually Diane hadn't been so quiet that day, she thought. Sara had been surprised to hear that bitingly sarcastic comment from the normally mild-mannered girl.

Sara felt tears suddenly spill down her cheeks. How could anyone have killed a sixteen-year-old girl? The whole thing was so tragic—and so terrifying.

All afternoon Sara saw groups of students huddled in hushed conversations between classes. The news of Diane's death was sweeping like wildfire through the school, casting a pall over everyone's usual exuberance. And Sara felt herself going through the motions of moving from class to class as if she were in a daze.

When she ran into Julie outside Hands-On Econ just before last period, Julie said, "I still can hardly believe it about Diane. I've been thinking about it all day."

Sara nodded somberly. "Yeah, me too. It's so sad."

"And scary." Julie's voice was low. "I just wish they'd catch this guy."

The bell rang and the two of them took their seats, but the normally lively class seemed to drag. Even Ms. Brooks seemed affected by the uneasy atmosphere. She must have heard about Diane, Sara thought.

As soon as class was over, Sara and Julie headed for the student-council meeting. The twelve homeroom representatives, six class senators, and four student-body officers gathered in the room that was normally used for speech class. Instead of being lined up in rows, the chairs were arranged in a rough square so that everyone could see everyone else.

Sara absentmindedly smiled hello to the kids she knew while she mentally geared herself up to present her idea to the group as soon as the meeting started. When Mike sauntered in and gave her a big smile, she felt a little sick. She hadn't realized before then how much she'd been looking forward to sharing the experience of being on student council with him. It wasn't going to be much fun losing an election she'd just won and not coming to the meetings almost before she got started. Then she saw Ginger slide into her seat with a self-satisfied smile and her temper flared. If Melodie and Ginger hadn't cooked up this vindictive scheme to get her off council, she wouldn't be in this situation now.

Damien Weiss, the student-body president, came into the room, greeting various people as he moved over to one of the chairs and dumped his books on the floor beside it. Then he walked up to Sara. Sticking out his hand, he introduced himself and said cheerfully, "You must be Sara Langdon—you're the only person here I haven't known since I was in kindergarten. Welcome to the Overton student council."

Sara returned his smile. "Nice to meet you," she said, trying to match his enthusiasm. But she felt like a fool. Wait till he hears what I have to say, she thought unhappily, and wondered if she was making a mistake.

Damien rapped his pencil on the edge of his desk to bring the meeting to order. "There are agendas here, so let's pass them around and get started."

Amid the rustling of paper, Sara took a deep breath and put up her hand. Damien looked at her in surprise. "Yes, Sara?"

"I have an item to bring up that is not on the agenda and I feel it needs to be said before the meeting begins." Sara swallowed nervously. All twenty-one pairs of eyes were staring at her. She clenched her hands together under the desktop and began. "Although I feel certain that the homeroom election I won was handled fairly, I have discovered that a number of people, some of them on this council, do not share that feeling."

Sara saw Ginger's mouth drop open in surprise. Now feeling a little more sure of herself, she went on. "Without the confidence of the entire student council I can't adequately represent the students in my homeroom. It isn't fair to them if people are suspicious about how the election was held."

Damien broke in, with a puzzled frown. "I don't understand what you mean."

Sara gave him a small smile. "To put it bluntly, some people think my election was rigged, that there's no way someone as new to Overton as I am could have won the election."

Mike's loud voice filled the room. "Wait a minute. That's the stupidest thing I've ever heard. How exactly do they think it was rigged? I mean, rigged elections for homeroom representative? Give me a break!"

There was a flurry of excited comments around the room and Damien rapped again on his desk for order. "Sara, could you explain?"

Sara shrugged. "I don't know how I'm supposed to have cheated, but that's what some people are saying."

"And you're suggesting we should try and stop these rumors?" Damien asked, looking a little dismayed.

"No, no," Sara said quickly. She took a deep breath. "I'm suggesting that my homeroom election be held again, right away, tomorrow morning. You can send observers from the student council to hand out and collect the ballots."

"Well," Damien said slowly, "it's pretty unusual. But I guess there's nothing wrong with it exactly. I mean, if you think a revote will settle things."

Ginger spoke up, her voice full of spite. "Yeah, sure, and then she and her friends will be on the phone all night, telling people . . ." Her words trailed off uncertainly as she saw everyone staring at her.

"No, that's exactly what's not going to happen," Sara said, the color rising in her cheeks. "In fact, no one in my homeroom will even know there's going to be a new election until class tomorrow morning if everyone in this room can promise not to say anything about it."

There was a babble of excited comment following Sara's statement and Damien banged a book on his desk in frustration. "That's enough," he said when the room had quieted down. Then, looking pointedly at Ginger, he went on. "There are undercurrents here that I don't even want to know about. But as far as I can see, Sara's plan is perfectly fine." He glanced at Sara and smiled. "I'll make the arrangements with Mrs. Lugano." His glance swept the room. "We all agree that this discussion does not leave this room. And I'm going to hold everyone here responsible for keeping it to themselves. Now, let's get on to the regular agenda."

One of the twelfth-grade representatives spoke up. "So, does Sara stay for this meeting, or what?"

"Sara stays. She's the elected representative until further notice." Damien's tone allowed for no opposition. With a stern look that included the whole room, he picked up his agenda and read the first item aloud.

Half an hour later the meeting was drawing to an end. When Damien asked if anyone had other new business to bring up, Nina Phelps, one of the tenth-grade senators, raised her hand.

"I hate to bring this up," she said nervously, "but I've been hearing rumors all day—" She swallowed convulsively. "Rumors about Diane Wallace being found murdered."

Sara could almost feel the shiver of fear that ran through the room. Her own hands were cold as ice. The word "murder" echoed in her brain.

Nina gulped again and said, "I'm really scared, and I think a lot of other people in this school are scared too. What can we do to protect ourselves? Shouldn't we start some kind of buddy system or something—you know, like they have when you go swimming at camp?"

No one laughed, and after a moment Damien said quietly, "I guess everyone has heard the rumor, and I'm afraid it's true, although I don't think anything official has been said yet. But Mr. Donahue caught me just before this meeting, and he's planning to have a schoolwide assembly sometime tomorrow. Someone from the police will be there, and they're going to be talking about safety issues. Probably they'll announce some information about the funeral too. But in the meantime we should all be extra careful."

Damien glanced at his watch. "I'm sorry to end this meeting on such a sad note, but we really do need to close it up now." There was a general shuffling of papers and books as the students prepared to leave. Damien's voice rose above the din. "Before you go, let me remind you that Nina's suggestion about a buddy system is a good one. None of you girls should be going anywhere alone. I have my car here and I'll be happy to give anyone a ride home who needs one, but under no circumstances should any of you walk home by yourselves. Let's not have any more tragedies."

CHAPTER 12

The minute the meeting was over, Mike jumped up and walked quickly over to where Sara was sitting. "What was all that about?" he demanded. "Who said there was some funny business about your election?"

Standing up, Sara looked into his stormy brown eyes and smiled softly. "It's too complicated to go into, Mike, and besides, it's over. I'm sure it will all get handled tomorrow morning."

Mike looked up at the big clock on the wall. "I've gotta get to practice, but I'll call you tonight, okay?"

When Sara nodded, he gave her shoulders a quick squeeze and then moved rapidly toward the door, still shaking his head in confusion. Watching him, Sara thought, I told him everything would get handled tomorrow, but I'm not so sure it will get worked out the way I hope.

She felt a little pang of regret; probably she wouldn't be part of the student council after the revote in the morning.

"Sara!" Damien's voice broke into her thoughts. She turned to find him looking at her with a smile. "I just wanted to tell you—I'll talk to Mrs. Lugano and tell her about holding the election over again, so when you get to homeroom tomorrow, it'll all be ready to go." He paused. "I'm really sorry you're having such a tough start to your student council career—but I'm sure everything will work out fine."

Julie was standing beside Sara, and she nodded her head vigorously. "Yeah, I'm sure it will."

"Now, do you two need a ride somewhere?" Damien was obviously taking his own warnings seriously.

Sara exchanged a glance with Julie. "Why don't you walk home with me, Julie?" She looked at the clock. "It's not even three-thirty yet. Then someone can give you a ride to your house later on."

As Julie nodded Damien said, "Okay, good. Just don't take any chances."

A few minutes later the two girls were walking along the leaf-strewn sidewalk. The brilliant sunshine all day had dried the puddles of water left by last night's storm, and the air felt clean and crisp. Sara watched a yellow leaf flutter slowly to the ground. These seasonal changes were so different from what she was used to at home in California, and she smiled to herself—she was secretly looking forward to snow.

"Well, that went really well." Julie's words brought Sara back to reality.

"Damien's awfully nice," Sara responded. "I can see why he was elected student-body president."

"Yeah, he is nice," Julie said. "He was plenty amazed at what you said."

"I was scared to death," Sara confessed.

"You sure didn't sound scared," Julie told her positively. "And everybody was wondering what it was all about—except Ginger, of course. Did you see the look on her face? You really caught her by surprise, and she couldn't do one thing about it. She went storming out of that meeting with steam coming out of her ears!"

Sara laughed, as Julie rushed on. "Our phones are going to be ringing off the hook tonight. It's pretty hard to keep a secret in this place. What are you going to say when people ask you what this was all about?" She looked at Sara.

"I don't plan to say anything," Sara replied in a definite tone. "None of us are."

"Oh, it's going to be so hard," Julie wailed. Then she caught Sara's expression and hastily added, "But of course, I promised and my lips are sealed—at least until tomorrow!" They both laughed and then Julie said with glee, "I can't wait to hear what Melodie's got to say. I'll bet she goes truly crazy. And it'll be her own fault, for starting something like this. She's going to be so sorry when you win that election again. It'll serve her right."

Sara sighed. It was so like Julie to be bubbling over with confidence. Sara wished it was contagious; she could use some of that enthusiasm right now. But she had to face the fact that even though she knew the first election was fair, other people might have been persuaded by Melodie and Ginger's insinuations that somehow it had been fixed. She guessed it was pretty surprising that someone brand new to the school, like her, had beaten Dick Stone, who had lived in Overton all his life. And besides, everyone knew that Sara was only going to be in Overton for a year.

Now that she thought about it, it was truly amazing—and flattering too—that she'd won the election. Sara wondered now if her success had really been based on Julie's popularity. Her friend's enthusiastic support, in the midst of her own whirlwind campaign, had probably been the factor that made people vote for Sara. Tomorrow it will be a different story, she decided sadly. One without that happy ending for me.

They turned a corner and ahead of them the street stretched deserted and empty. No one was outside in the late-afternoon sunshine, and there wasn't a single car moving along the road. Sara felt a small shiver run down her spine. The thought of Diane Wallace's murder slid into her mind. How could anyone be killed in such a pretty place?

As if sensing Sara's thoughts, Julie glanced briefly over her shoulder, back along the deserted street. "It's kind of creepy, isn't it?" she said in a low voice. Without waiting for an answer, she unconsciously quickened her pace, and the two of them hurried toward the safety of Sara's house.

Aunt Liz was home and wonderful smells were coming from the kitchen. "Hi, honey," Liz said, giving Sara a hug. "And Julie, it's good to see you. I hope you'll be able to stay for dinner. I got back earlier than I'd expected and fell right into a cooking frenzy."

Julie and Sara laughed. "Sure, that sounds great," Julie said. "I'll call my mom and let her know I'll be home after dinner."

"Good," Aunt Liz said. "Now come on into the kitchen and pick up a snack to hold you over. I know you girls can eat everything in sight without ever filling up." She patted her own flat stomach. "I wish I could still keep up with you." As she loaded two plates she asked, "Are you going to work on that finance class you're taking together? It sounds like such a good idea—they sure didn't have anything like that when I was in school. I had to struggle to learn it all on my own."

Julie grinned. "Well, the only time I even get a clue about what's going on in that class is when

Sara explains it to me." Then the two of them trooped up the stairs to Sara's room, balancing their snacks and books precariously.

As they sat down to dinner Aunt Liz asked, "So, did anything exciting happen at school today?"

Before either Sara or Julie could say anything, Uncle Ted spoke up. "I guess a girl from school getting raped and murdered could count as exciting news."

Aunt Liz gasped. "What? A girl from school?"

Sara nodded slowly. While they'd been doing homework she'd managed to push the horrible thought of Diane's murder out of her conscious mind, but Uncle Ted's words brought it flooding back. "Yes," she told her aunt, "her name was Diane Wallace."

"But what happened? Did you know her? Oh, this is terrible."

"I knew her a little bit," Sara said.

"She was a nice girl." Julie shook her head. "I mean, I've known her since she moved to Overton in the third grade. I just can't believe she's dead."

"Oh, dear." Aunt Liz's voice was full of distress. "She couldn't have been more than sixteen if she was in your grade—what a terrible thing to happen. And her poor family. Does anyone know who did it or how it happened?"

"Well, no one has seen her since Monday. A bunch of us went out that night after the school election," Julie explained. "Diane was supposed to join us, but she never showed up. Then the next day we heard that she left her house that evening and just disappeared." Julie sighed. "Her mom and dad are divorced and her mom was really worried about her."

"I can imagine," Aunt Liz said, her eyes wide with fear. "But—"

"A couple of guys found her in the river today. I guess her body was caught in some branches under the bridge," Sara said quickly, wanting not to have to think about the gruesome details. "But LuAnn said—her dad's a cop—that she wasn't killed where she was found. They don't know where it happened."

Aunt Liz sighed sadly and Uncle Ted said in a jokey voice, "Well, I know where I'd kill someone—Uncle Jack's old derelict barn out on Smithtown Road never has anyone around it. Total privacy."

"Oh, Ted," Aunt Liz said with a shake of her head. "This isn't anything to joke about." She saw Sara and Julie's puzzled expressions. "Ted inherited some family property outside of town, and he keeps saying he wants to sell it, but so far it hasn't happened. I'm not sure he doesn't secretly want to hold on to it."

"Meanwhile old Jim Johnson keeps the hay cut and the weeds under control," Uncle Ted said. "He's a weird guy—maybe it's him that killed your friend."

"Ted, that's enough!" Aunt Liz told him sharply. Then she looked at Sara and Julie. "You girls must be so upset. It's just heartbreaking."

During the rest of the meal everyone seemed determined to keep off the subject of the murder, but the conversation was filled with awkward silences, and Sara was relieved when it was over. Pushing back his chair, Uncle Ted said, "Well, Julie, let me know when you're ready to go home and I'll give you a ride."

"Thanks anyway, Mr. Martin, but my mom is coming by for me in a little while," Julie told him. "She's got to go out to pick up the medicine the doctor ordered for my dad. The prescription's supposed to be ready by eight."

After Sara said good night to her friend and watched as Julie ran out and got into her mom's car, she trudged up the stairs to her room. The house was quiet—Uncle Ted was reading in the living room and Aunt Liz was working on her decorator business accounts in the kitchen. Sara closed her door behind her and shivered. What was going on in Overton? It felt like some kind of menace had invaded the small ordinary town, and it seemed to be coming closer.

CHAPTER 13

Thirty seconds before the bell rang, Sara walked into Mrs. Lugano's homeroom the next morning. She had purposely not gotten to school early, because she didn't want to talk to anyone about the new election that would be held first thing. Contrary to Julie's predictions, there hadn't been a tidal wave of calls last night to discuss it— Sara was glad, because she wouldn't have known what to say. It had been hard enough talking to Mike and telling him she couldn't answer all his questions. Now she just wanted to get it over with. In fact, she admitted to herself that maybe she should have just left the whole business alone and not asked to have a revote. After all, what could Melodie and Ginger have done? Probably no one would have believed their tales of rigged elections and stuffed ballot boxes, and Sara could have stayed on the student council. But it was too late now.

Mrs. Lugano took attendance and then said, "We have some business to take care of this morning, and I'm going to let Damien Weiss tell you about it."

Damien walked up to the front of the room. "Here's the problem. Some people have suggested that there was something wrong with the election for student council representative from this homeroom. So we're going to hold the election again right now." He picked up some papers from Mrs. Lugano's desk.

Before Damien got any further, Dick Stone said in a loud voice, "I think a lot of us know what these rumors are and who started them. And I think it's a disgusting bunch of garbage." His gaze swept the room. "If we're going to hold another vote, let's make it unanimous. Everyone in favor of Sara Langdon as our homeroom representative, raise your hand."

Dick's hand shot up as he finished speaking. Sara looked at the other students and saw that everyone's hand but hers was up in the air.

"Come on, Sara," Dick said with a smile, "we want it to be really unanimous—no abstentions."

Self-consciously Sara raised her hand, and a chorus of "Way to go!" and "All right!" swirled around her. Dick turned back to Damien, who still stood at the front of the room. "There's your vote."

Damien smiled. "Thanks for making things so easy, everyone. See you around." As he left the room he dropped the stack of unused ballots into the wastebasket by the door.

Sinking back in her seat, Sara thought, What a nice bunch of kids. I'm lucky to have ended up in this homeroom. She remembered thinking when she'd walked in that first day of school that the class was filled mainly with kids that weren't in the most popular groups—boring serious souls who did nothing but study, and definitely not the star athletes and social butterflies. And maybe that was true, she reflected now, but they'd been a lot better friends to her than popular people like Melodie and Ginger. As she walked out the door she smiled at Dick, who was right behind her. "Thanks a lot, Dick."

He grinned back at her. "Hey, Sara, you won fair and square the first time, no matter what anyone pretends to think. I was just helping things along." With a wave he turned down the hall toward the library.

Julie had caught up with Sara and now she flung the arm that wasn't full of books around her friend. "What did I tell you?" she crowed. "Now let's see what those nasty little schemers have to say."

The warm glow of acceptance stayed with Sara all morning, and by lunchtime everyone seemed to have heard the whole story. She was turning the combination on her locker when Mike came up behind her and hugged her hard. "I guess you're going to be on student council after all," he said softly, "no thanks to my ex-friend Melodie Burton." He paused, and Sara saw a steely glint in his eyes. "I wouldn't have liked to be in her shoes if things hadn't worked out okay."

Sara smiled at him. "But it did work out, so that's the end of it."

Mike smiled back. "Right. Listen, Sara, about tonight, I forgot that I have to go to a birthday dinner for my grandma—she's in a nursing home in Youngstown, so it's basically the whole evening. Besides, I have to get to bed fairly early because of the game tomorrow. You're coming to the game, right?" Sara nodded, and he went on. "Great. Plan to hang around after it's over and we'll go out for pizza to celebrate."

"You're pretty sure there'll be something to celebrate," Sara teased him.

"You got it." Mike's grin lit up his whole face, and Sara felt her heart skip a beat.

Right after lunch everyone filed into the auditorium for the all-school assembly. The man in uniform on the stage must be Overton's police chief, Sara thought, and the realization of the reason for this assembly washed over her again in a cold wave.

When Mr. Donahue, the high-school principal, started to talk, the auditorium was completely silent. He confirmed what they all knew—Diane had been strangled, and her body had been found in the river just outside town, but the police believed she had been killed somewhere else.

Chief Patterson talked only about safety—
Sara got the impression that he didn't want to
tell the students any details about the murder.
She shivered involuntarily—could the police possibly think that one of the high-school kids might
be the killer?

Sara listened as the chief warned female students and teachers to be especially careful. "The
most important thing is not to go anywhere
alone—not even to school if you can help it. We
think this incident happened in the evening or
at night, but until we catch this person, it's best
to take no chances. Go with a friend, a parent,
anyone you know you can trust. Best of all, go in
a group."

We all know better than to go out alone at
night, Sara thought. I wish they'd hurry up and
catch this guy.

When Chief Patterson had finished, Mr. Donahue told them that a memorial service for Diane
would be held next Tuesday afternoon at two
o'clock. "Mrs. Wallace asked me to tell you that
you are all welcome to be there. Anyone who
wishes to attend will be released early from
school—please tell your homeroom teacher on
Tuesday morning." He went on to remind the
students to report any suspicious incidents to
the police, as the chief had requested. "And
now, before you leave, I'd like to ask for a
minute of silence while we remember Diane
Wallace."

Filing up the aisles to the exits, everyone looked serious and sad. Some of the girls were sniffling, and Marsha's face was blotched with tears. As she stood outside in the hall Sara saw Rick coming out the auditorium's other door. Remembering how she'd run away from him in the library and then found his threatening note in her book, she decided, If something like that happens again, I'm going to report it.

She thought of the gutsy way Diane had shut Rick up when he'd tormented Sara last week in history class, and her eyes smarted with tears. Poor Diane—how terrified she must have been! Could Rick have been so angry at her put-down that he'd killed her? Sara didn't want to believe that a person she actually knew was a murderer, but someone had strangled Diane Wallace.

The memorial assembly for Diane had used up the whole class period after lunch, when Sara normally had chemistry. Since Friday was a gym day, she headed for the girls' locker room only to find Mrs. Hernandez, the gym instructor, as sniffly and sad-faced as everyone else.

"Let's put on our warm-ups and take a nice brisk walk outside today, ladies," Mrs. Hernandez told them. Her eyes were still teary and she took a moment to blow her nose and then went on. "I doubt that any of us is in the mood for competitive sports today. But some exercise will help work off a little of the tension and sadness."

Even the normally businesslike Ms. Brooks was subdued when Sara arrived at her Hands-On Econ class. Instead of piling on homework because a weekend was coming up, Ms. Brooks suggested they all reexamine their budgets and lists of assets and liabilities. "On Monday we'll begin investing with our imaginary portfolios. Some of you might want to try a few of these investments for real later on. But for now, let's keep it all on paper until everyone has a grasp of how the various investments work," she said just as class ended.

Julie grinned at Sara as the two of them headed out into the hall. "I hope she doesn't plan to wait until everyone in the class understands what she's talking about. Then nobody would get to try these fabulous investments anytime in the foreseeable future."

"Oh, Julie, you'll be up to speed in no time," Sara told her. "Wait and see. It's just like anything else—one day it's a total mystery and the next day it's suddenly clear as can be."

"Right," Julie said with a laugh. "Well, I'm definitely still in the fogbound stage."

Sara laughed with her and they started walking toward their lockers.

The next day was bright and crisp, perfect weather for football. This time Marsha had managed to get the use of her mom's car to take a bunch of the girls over to Trenton for the game. As Sara climbed into the backseat she once again

longed for the freedom of driving. Her birthday
was only a month away. So far, every time she
brought up the subject of getting her driver's
license, Uncle Ted went through a whole routine
about how dangerous teenage drivers were and
how expensive it was to insure them. He'd point
out that Sara was their responsibility while she
was living with them and then ask her if she had
ever had transportation difficulties since she'd
arrived.

Sara felt stuck between a rock and a hard
place. If she complained, then she felt ungrate-
ful for all the kind things they did for her. And
besides, then Uncle Ted would redouble his offers
to drive her places. If she agreed that she was
getting around fine, then he'd give her his "so
what's the problem?" look.

Even Aunt Liz wasn't much help. She kind of
tuned out when Uncle Ted was on one of his cru-
sades. Probably it was easier to ignore him than
to try to change his mind. Sara had tried having
a heart-to-heart talk with Aunt Liz, but her aunt
had managed to change the conversation as soon
as she saw where it was headed. It was almost
as if Aunt Liz was afraid to go head-to-head with
Uncle Ted on this issue or any other.

Up until now Sara hadn't had a chance to
say much on the subject to her dad during his
periodic phone calls. The calls were often rushed,
since her dad had to travel a long way to get to
a phone and usually there was a line of people

behind him waiting to use it. By the time he'd asked how Sara was and told her he was fine and spoken a moment to Aunt Liz, he was feeling pressured to give up his turn at the precious link to the outside world.

As the carful of Overton High junior girls maneuvered onto the highway to Trenton, Sara decided that she would write to her dad and explain the situation to him that way. Surely he'd see that to be sixteen and not be allowed to drive was pretty much the worst thing that could happen to anyone.

CHAPTER 14

The pregame pep rally was already under way by the time Sara and the rest of the girls climbed into the bleachers overlooking the football field at Trenton High. Across the way masses of Trenton students were practicing the Trenton Tiger roar.

Julie had managed to get people to scoot over enough that there was room for all five of them—Julie, LuAnn, Marsha, Shari, and Sara—halfway up the stands near the fifty-yard line. Leave it to Julie, Sara thought, to find us the best seats in the place. There was a perfect view of the field and Sara could see Mike warming up with the rest of his team. He must have been watching for her, because as soon as she settled into her seat on the aisle, he threw a grin right at her.

The Trenton Tigers and the Overton Bulldogs were long-standing rivals, and when Mike made the first touchdown, Sara screamed with enthusiasm. The Bulldogs made the extra point and the Overton side of the field went wild. But the Tigers weren't about to be beaten. By halftime both teams had scored three touchdowns and had managed to make two of their three tries at the extra point; the score was even at twenty to twenty.

The game stayed tied through most of the third quarter. Neither side was willing to take a chance on an interception, so they slogged it out on the ground with no one getting near to either end zone. Sara's voice was almost nonexistent, her throat raw from yelling encouragement to Mike and the other players. Then, shortly after the fourth quarter began, the Tigers surged ahead with a touchdown and then a field goal.

"Don't worry, Sara," Julie yelled when she saw the look of concern on her friend's face. "Our guys are tough and really determined. That's why they're called Bulldogs!"

Just then a fight broke out on the field, and soon most of the players from both teams were piled in a struggling, punching mass on the Bulldogs' thirty-yard line. The refs blew their whistles, and for a few moments there was quiet in the stands as students nervously watched the players get untangled from one another and limp off the field. Sara held her breath as Mike struggled out from the middle of the pile, but he didn't seem at all hurt as he trotted back to his position on the field.

Now it was the Bulldogs' ball. For a moment Sara couldn't tell where the ball was. Then she saw Mike tuck it into the crook of his arm and plow through the line of Tigers trying to stop him. "Way to go, Mike!" she yelled.

"Oh, yeah, way to go, Mikey baby," a sarcastic voice said in Sara's ear. Melodie was standing in the aisle beside her, a soft drink in her hand.

Sara turned to stare at Melodie and in that moment saw a look of pure hatred in the other girl's eyes. Then, with a casual flip of her wrist, Melodie splashed her soft drink out of its cup. The sticky liquid ran down Sara's head and soaked the side of her sweater and shirt. "Oh, my gosh, I'm so sorry," Melodie said, sounding totally insincere. "I hope you don't catch pneumonia or something in those wet clothes."

Marsha was sitting beside Sara and she glared at Melodie. "You did that on purpose," she said angrily.

Melodie shrugged. "Look, accidents happen. I said I was sorry." She gave Sara a mean grin and then ran down the bleacher steps to her seat a few rows closer to the field.

By this time Julie and LuAnn noticed what was going on and so did Dick Stone, who was sitting behind them. Julie glared in Melodie's direction. "What a snake! You should have pushed her down the stairs, Sara." She moved over and started dabbing at Sara's hair and sweater with some paper napkins. "You're really soaked. That witch!"

Dick nodded. "Definitely not a nice thing to do. But no one's ever accused Melodie of being a nice person." He handed Sara the blanket he'd been sitting on. "Here, you better put this around you or you'll freeze."

Sara's teeth had already begun to chatter and she gratefully hugged the blanket around her. Although the afternoon sun was still bright, the air was cold. The sticky, wet fabric of her clothes clung to her skin and felt disgusting. Even her hair was drenched, dripping the cold, sugary liquid down her neck.

Sara watched as the Bulldogs made a touchdown and scored their extra point. She was glad her team was closing the gap, but she felt too miserable to enjoy herself. In spite of the blanket wrapped around her shoulders, Sara was still shivering and she could just imagine how terrible she looked.

Finally, with five minutes left to play, Mike scored another touchdown for the Bulldogs and put them in the lead. Marsha and the others were totally engrossed in the game and showed no signs of wanting to leave. Dick Stone leaned his head down near Sara's. "You look really miserable. Why don't I take you home? I think the Bulldogs have it all wrapped up at this point and I'm ready to go."

Sara shot him a grateful look. "Thanks, Dick. Even with your blanket I'm beginning to feel like a Popsicle. I just hope I don't drip all over your car," she added with a grin. Then she said to Julie and Marsha, "I've got to get out of here and Dick's leaving anyway. If you see Mike, tell him I'll catch up with him at Jake's later."

Uncle Ted's car was gone, but Aunt Liz was home when Dick dropped Sara off a short time later. Sara asked her aunt if she could have a ride over to the pizza place after she changed, and then she went up to the bathroom and peeled off her wet clothes.

A hot shower and freshly shampooed hair made Sara feel like a new person. The whole time she was getting dressed her mind alternated between trying to think up ways of getting even with Melodie and telling herself that revenge was only for the meanspirited.

Aunt Liz pulled up in front of Jake's pizza place and Sara could see that the parking lot was jammed. She waved goodbye to her aunt and moved toward the heavy double doors that led inside. But as she reached for the door handle she hesitated. She felt awkward walking into a crowded place all by herself. Come on, Sara, don't be a dummy, she said half aloud. Mike's inside and he'll be glad to see you.

Jake's was packed with students and the smell of garlic-laden pizza was almost overpowering. Sara spotted Mike halfway across the main room and worked her way over to his side.

"Hi," she said shyly.

"Hi yourself," Mike responded, but without his usual welcoming grin. "I'm kind of surprised you made it. When I didn't see you after the game—"

"Didn't Julie tell you what happened? I had to go home and change."

Mike scowled. "I didn't see Julie. I was too busy looking for you. I don't know why you thought changing your clothes was more important than coming here with me. I thought you looked fine in what you had on at the game."

Sara sighed. She was about to explain when Julie and Marsha appeared, each of them clutching a soft drink in one hand and a slice of pizza in the other. "Sara, are you okay?" Julie asked. Without waiting for a response, Julie turned to Mike. "You better put that ex-girlfriend of yours on a leash, Mike."

"What are you talking about?" he demanded to know.

Marsha leaped in with a vivid account of what Melodie had done at the game. "You should have seen Sara. She was absolutely soaked from head to toe," Marsha finished, with only a slight exaggeration.

Mike turned to Sara. "She really did that? I mean, I knew she was a little upset, but this is crazy." The angry expression on his face made Sara wince. "Well, she's not going to pull a stunt like that again. I'll make sure of it."

"Oh, Mike," Sara said quietly, looping her arm through his. "It could have been an accident. Besides, it wasn't a big deal." She wiggled her fingers goodbye to Julie and Marsha and drew Mike toward the counter. "Come on, let's get some pizza."

Listen to me—Melodie's protector, she thought as the two of them got slices and drinks and then threaded their way toward the booths in the back. Sara'd been plenty angry with Melodie at the time, but when he heard about the incident, Mike had looked like he could actually strangle her.

By the time Sara was totally stuffed with pizza, she'd heard the replay of every moment of the game. Mike's friends on the team kept stopping by their booth, and with each new arrival, another fabulous play had to be reenacted. Finally Mike said to Sara, "Come on, let's get out of here. How about a movie? Anything you want to see?"

Sara smiled up at him as he put his arm around her shoulders. "Well, there are four screens at the mall, so there's bound to be something that's watchable."

On the way home after the movie Mike took a detour and drove out past the fairgrounds. The few security floodlights cast shadows across the buildings and open stretches of ground. The main gate had a big chain and padlock on it, but

Mike drove down the access road along the fence until they came to another, smaller gate. "Feel like taking a walk?" he asked.

Sara looked at the gate and then back at Mike. "Sure," she said, "but this gate's locked too."

Mike laughed. "Oh, that. It just looks locked. Everyone in Overton must know how to jiggle the padlock and open it up. I think the locks are just to keep the out-of-towners from using it when the fairgrounds are closed."

Sure enough, Mike fiddled with the sturdy-looking padlock for a moment and the gate swung open. Soon the two of them were crunching through the fallen leaves that covered the deserted fairgrounds.

Hand in hand, Mike and Sara wandered past the closed and boarded-up animal barns. "You didn't get here early enough this summer to come to the fair, did you?" Mike asked. Sara shook her head and he went on. "I guess every town has some place that's special— a place with special memories for every kid who's grown up there. Maybe it's a swimming pool or the farm where you go for horseback riding and hayrack rides. But in Overton, it's the fairgrounds. Did you know that the Overton fair is the biggest one in this part of the state?"

Sara laughed. "No, I have to confess I didn't know that."

"It probably seems like pretty small potatoes to someone from L.A., but this old fairgrounds has a lot of great memories for me." He shook his head with a grin. "Can you believe that I still have the blue ribbon I won for building the best birdhouse when I was ten? And I can remember when I entered Elvis in the dog show one summer."

"Did he win?" Sara asked.

"Well, not really. He was the weirdest-looking dog—part bassett, part collie—and one of his legs was shorter than the others, so he kind of wiggled when he walked. Anyway, they gave him a trophy for 'most unusual.' I thought it was terrific at the time."

Sara squeezed Mike's hand. "Sounds like Overton was a great town to grow up in."

"Yeah, I guess," Mike said slowly. Then he slid his arm around Sara's shoulders and kissed the top of her head. "You know, Sara, you're really good for me," he told her. "The last time I was out here, it was because I was so worked up over something that I had to run all the way around the perimeter fence twice before I cooled down. And now here I am with you, all mellowed out and talking about a lot of dumb stuff from when I was a kid instead of thinking about how I'd like to punch somebody's lights out."

For a few moments they walked along in silence, then Mike went on. "I don't know why I have such a terrible temper, but sometimes things get to me and I just see red. Like when I heard that stunt Mel pulled."

"Hey, it's over," Sara said softly. "And I didn't shrink or dissolve or anything."

"Nope, you didn't," he said, pulling her close. "You're still just the right size. But I've got to tell you something about Mel and me."

Sara stiffened. Great, she thought, this is what I get for being a good sport—he's going to tell me that he's going back with her.

"The night after the election, when I told you I was going out with the guys? Well, that's not exactly what happened," Mike confessed. "I'd planned to go with them, but Mel got hold of me and said she had to see me and she sounded really sad, so I took her for a ride instead. That's why, when you asked if Rick was with us that evening, I didn't know what to say."

Sara waited a long moment, and when Mike didn't go on, she finally asked, "So what happened with you and Melodie?"

She felt Mike's muscles tighten at the memory. "Nothing much. I guess Mel decided it was time for the two of us to get back together." His voice was low and cold, as if he was trying to keep his anger from erupting. "She doesn't look at people as human beings. She sees them as possessions to keep or toss away. Last summer she unloaded me like a piece of trash, but now she thinks she made a mistake and she figures I'll go along with whatever her current plan is. Someday someone is going to teach Mel a serious lesson about human relationships."

The words sounded like a threat and Sara shivered. She glanced around at the dark and empty fairgrounds and then up at Mike's towering frame. His mouth was a grim angry line. Wow, she thought, I sure hope Melodie doesn't run into Mike in a deserted place like this some night.

By the time Mike took Sara home, his mood had lightened. But the tension of the past hour had affected Sara and she wasn't happy to see Uncle Ted rise out of his easy chair as she came in the front door.

"You know it's past midnight," he said, pointing to his watch. "Where were you all this time?"

Sara bit back the smart-aleck reply that was on her lips. Instead she said, "I had pizza at Jake's and then Mike gave me a ride home." She paused for a moment as she saw his scowl deepen. Then she took a deep breath, deciding it was time to show him she was adult enough to explain her point of view calmly and rationally. "Look, Uncle Ted, I'm sorry if you were worried about me. But it's Saturday night. You know, we're all being really careful since they found Diane—you don't have to be concerned."

Uncle Ted just stared at her. "You seem to think I'm being unfair, Sara. And I know you're not one of those smartmouth kids who hang out at the Tavern like that Diane girl. But you're a very beautiful young woman—I'm sure you're well aware of that." He paused, his expression unreadable. "And men can be dangerous."

A silence stretched out between them—Sara didn't have any idea what to say. At last Uncle Ted said gruffly, "I'm going to stay up and watch the end of this movie. See you in the morning."

Sara ran up the stairs, feeling absurdly relieved. The conversation had made her uncomfortable in a way she couldn't explain, and she wanted to put it out of her mind. The other bedroom door was open and the light was on inside. Sara stuck her head in and saw her aunt propped up in bed reading a book.

Aunt Liz glanced up and smiled. Putting down the book, she opened her arms for a hug. "Hi, honey," she said. "Did you have fun tonight?"

Sure I did, Sara thought as she leaned over to hug her aunt. So far I've found out that my boyfriend has a murderous temper and I've had a totally weird conversation with my uncle. But other than that the evening was great.

CHAPTER 15

Tuesday, the day of Diane Wallace's funeral, dawned bright and chilly. Most of the juniors and many of the other students planned to attend the service and wore their best dark-colored clothes to school. The mood throughout the morning was somber as everyone thought ahead to what the afternoon would bring.

But as Sara and Julie were sitting down at a lunch table, LuAnn came running up with a big grin on her face. "I just talked to my mom," she said, sliding into a chair next to Sara's. "It looks like they've caught the ski-mask rapist!"

"No kidding?" Julie responded. "That's great news."

"Not that it helps Diane any at this point," Sara reminded them. "But at least her mom might feel a little better knowing they caught the man who killed her. Are they sure it's the right guy?"

LuAnn nodded. "Oh, yeah. Of course, Marlene didn't see the guy's face who raped her, but the rest of him fits her description. But the real thing is, they've found the ski mask and they've got some kind of physical evidence that links him to Marlene." She leaned closer to the other two girls. "Of course, my dad won't tell me exactly what it is, but he says they've got this guy dead to rights. No way is he going to slip out of this."

"Who is he?" Julie wanted to know.

LuAnn looked around to see who was sitting within hearing distance. "I'm not really supposed to say until they've made a public announcement." Then she lowered her voice even more. "His name is Lee Dumling and he's a thirty-year-old construction worker in Trenton. He already has a record for assaults against women in Michigan. And get this— he's married! Can you imagine suddenly finding out that your husband was a rapist and a killer?"

Satisfied that she'd totally amazed her friends, LuAnn stood up and put her finger to her lips. "Remember, don't breathe a word until you see it on the news. I'm going to go get something to eat. Be right back."

Watching LuAnn walk to the cafeteria line, Sara couldn't suppress a smile. "I wonder if LuAnn's dad realizes that every word he utters comes directly to the Overton High lunchroom," she said to Julie. "She must carry pockets full of change and spend half her time at the pay phone in the school lobby."

"Oh, LuAnn's okay," Julie said. "She just can't get over the fact that her dad's a cop." But she grinned too.

Somehow LuAnn, Julie, and Sara managed to keep the information about Lee Dumling to themselves for the rest of the afternoon. As she left the church Sara searched Mrs. Wallace's face for signs that Diane's poor mother had heard about her daughter's killer being captured. But the woman was almost overcome with grief. "So good of you kids to come today," she kept saying over and over.

Sara didn't know Diane or her mom that well, so she stood by awkwardly while Marsha and Julie gave the woman a hug. "Look at how many kids came," Mrs. Wallace said in some amazement. "I had no idea how popular Diane was." Then she smiled at the three girls in front of her. "But I always knew she had a nice group of friends."

Julie had borrowed her mom's car for the day and had driven Sara and a bunch of the other girls to the funeral. LuAnn was dropped off first on the way home, and as she left the car she winked at Sara and Julie. "I guess I'll talk to you later," she told them. "I'm going to see what's on the early news."

"Wasn't being at the funeral in person enough?" Marsha asked with a sniffle as they watched LuAnn trot up her front side-walk. "Does she really plan to watch clips of it on TV?"

Julie and Sara looked at each other but didn't say anything. Marsha went on. "It was really great that so many kids from school went to the funeral. I think it made Mrs. Wallace feel a lot better."

"I had no idea she was that popular," Sara said quietly. "She didn't seem to be around all that much."

Julie glanced at Marsha and then said, "Well, Diane had another group of friends too—guys from down at the Tavern. She spent a fair amount of time there. But her mom didn't know and I'm glad they didn't show up."

As soon as the last of the girls had been dropped off, Sara asked Julie, "Do you really think there'll be something on the news about the killer being arrested?"

Julie grinned. "I've never known LuAnn to be wrong about that kind of thing yet. Let's go to your house and turn on the TV!"

Wonderful odors were coming from the kitchen when they got there. Sara could tell that Aunt Liz was in another cooking frenzy. "Want to stay for dinner, Julie?" Aunt Liz asked. "We're having sausage and peppers and onions, and there's plenty."

"Gee, yeah. If it's really okay," Julie said. "I'll just call my mom and tell her what I'm doing."

While Julie went to the phone Aunt Liz put her arm around Sara's shoulders and gave them a squeeze. "Was the funeral awful?" she asked.

Sara shook her head slowly. "Mostly it was just sad. But there were lots of kids from school there, so Mrs. Wallace felt pretty good about that."

"That's nice, honey," Aunt Liz said, and stroked her niece's hair.

Julie returned and Sara said with more enthusiasm, "But guess what! They've caught Diane's killer. I don't think the police told Mrs. Wallace yet, but when they do, that should make her feel better, shouldn't it?"

Aunt Liz smiled sadly at Sara. "Honey, I don't think there's anything in the world that can make a woman feel better about losing her child." Then she gave Sara another hug. "But I'm sure she'll be happy to know that the killer is behind bars and that no other mother will have to go through what she did."

The two girls went up to Sara's room to study until it was time for the local news on TV. When it came on, Aunt Liz joined them in the living room to watch. Sure enough, there was Lee Dumling trying to hold his hands in front of his face while he was being put into a police car. And all the information about him was exactly what LuAnn had told them.

Uncle Ted arrived home as the weather report came on. Aunt Liz went to the front door to greet him. As the two of them moved into the living room, Aunt Liz said, "Let me get you a drink while you sit here with the girls and watch the news. I'm sure they'll rerun it."

"Rerun what? Did World War Three break out and I missed hearing about it?" Uncle Ted asked good-naturedly.

"No," Aunt Liz said with a laugh as she went into the dining room to fetch a tray of snacks and drinks. "They've caught the man who killed Diane Wallace—you remember Sara and Julie's friend from school."

Surprised, Uncle Ted looked at Sara and Julie for confirmation. "No kidding," he said softly. "Well, that's really something." Then he took a slow sip of his drink. "So who is this guy?" he asked.

"Look," said Julie. "There he is." She grabbed the clicker out of Sara's hand and turned up the volume. After the story had rerun, Julie toned down the sound again and said fiercely, "I wish they'd cut his balls off before they electrocute him."

Uncle Ted almost spilled his drink and Aunt Liz gulped audibly. "Well, Julie, remind me never to have you on my jury," Uncle Ted said with a small laugh. Then his face became serious. Uh-oh, Sara thought, here comes the "innocent till proved guilty" lecture. Uncle Ted went on, his voice solemn now. "Let me remind you girls that this man was arrested, not convicted. Although if he did what they say—sneaked up on girls in the dark wearing a ski mask—then he deserves whatever he gets. No real man would resort to such a thing."

During dinner the conversation finally moved off the arrest of Lee Dumling and Diane's funeral. Sara had an idea for the student council that she'd been noodling over and decided that this was a good time to try it out. "What do you think of letting kids go off campus for lunch instead of having to eat it in the cafeteria?" she asked them all.

"I can't see what it would hurt," Aunt Liz said after a moment. "After all, the food they serve there probably isn't all that wonderful—at least it wasn't when I went to school. And I've discovered that taking a sack lunch really isn't the in thing to do," she went on, with a pointed look at Sara, who had steadfastly refused to take her lunch and let everyone think she was a geek.

Julie rolled her eyes. "Nobody takes a sack lunch," she said emphatically.

"Sara, I don't know where you come up with these ideas," Uncle Ted said, ignoring both Aunt Liz's and Julie's comments. "If kids left school in the middle of the day, who would make sure they came back?"

"Every class takes attendance, Uncle Ted. It's not a problem."

"Still," he argued, "you'd have a bunch of kids roaming around town. Who knows what sort of trouble they'd get into. Besides, it would encourage them to pile into cars and go riding off all over the place looking for somewhere to eat."

Sara sighed. "What do you think, Julie?"

"I think it's a great idea. But you'd never get it past the school administration," she said sadly.

Uncle Ted broke in. "Besides, if the food's so lousy at the cafeteria, who would eat there when kids could go somewhere else? They'd lose all your business. They're not fools, Sara."

Suddenly Sara had an inspiration. "What if we brought regular restaurants to the school, then?" To a chorus of "What do you mean?" she went on, thinking it out as she spoke. "Maybe some of the big chains would put food outlets into the cafeteria. They do that at universities—I know UCLA has a bunch of food stations with all sorts of stuff to eat."

"Sure, and they have about a million times the number of students that Overton does to support them," Uncle Ted pointed out. "I think you'd be better served to put your thinking energies to your homework and not worry about the choices of lunch food."

That put an effective end to the conversation, but Sara kept mulling the idea over in her mind. There was probably something that could be done if only she could figure out a solution that would please everyone.

"I have a small announcement to make," Aunt Liz said brightly, filling up the silence that had descended on the dinner table. "You know that new hotel they're planning to build in the industrial park on Mill Road? Well, I've been contacted to bid on decorating the entire hotel!"

"Wow, Aunt Liz, that's fabulous!" Sara exclaimed. "You'll get the job for sure, won't she, Uncle Ted?"

"Hey, slow down a minute, Sara," Aunt Liz said with a laugh. "I haven't even put together my presentation yet." Then she turned to her husband. "What do you think, Ted?"

Uncle Ted smiled at her reassuringly. "It's an honor to be asked to bid, but, Liz, it's a pretty big project. My guess is that they'll end up with one of the large firms they've used on other sites. After all, you're in business by yourself. What if you got sick or something?"

"Well, I'm going to make sure that my designs are so terrific that they won't be able to go with anyone else. And I don't carry the massive overhead those big decorating outfits have. My markups are less, so my overall price has to be lower."

"Don't forget that the big guys get better deals from the manufacturers. Not only do they deal in huge quantities, but they also have a steady stream of orders," Uncle Ted pointed out.

Aunt Liz stuck out her chin defiantly. "I have a good relationship with my suppliers. I think

I have a shot at it." She seemed undaunted by her husband's lack of enthusiasm and Sara wondered how her aunt kept up her self-confidence in the face of his continual pessimism. She glanced at Julie, who had a perplexed look on her face.

"Anyway," Aunt Liz went on, "what this means is that you two will have to fend for yourselves for a few days. I'm off to Cincinnati on Thursday. The preliminary meetings are on Friday, and I thought I'd ask Beth if I can stay with her—you remember Beth, don't you, Ted?" To Sara and Julie she explained, "Beth is an old friend from high school and college. She's got a law practice in Cincinnati and we hardly ever see each other. If she's free on Saturday, I'd like to hang around and do stuff with her and come home on Sunday."

"Sounds like fun," Sara told her aunt. "We'll manage fine, won't we, Uncle Ted?" she added, giving him a pointed look.

"Oh, sure. You go on and have a good time with your friend," Uncle Ted agreed. "But, Liz, I don't want you to get your hopes up too much about this job. I'm worried that you're setting yourself up for disappointment."

Later, as Sara was helping Julie gather up her stuff to leave, Julie said, "Gee, your uncle is really tough to take."

"Yeah, I know," Sara agreed. "He's always putting Aunt Liz's work down. I don't know how she manages to keep so cheerful and optimistic."

Julie hoisted her book bag to her shoulder. "Sounds to me like what he wants is some little wifey to stay home and bake cookies. Men!"

CHAPTER 16

The arrest of Lee Dumling on suspicion of rape and murder did much to lighten the spirits of students at Overton High. Although many of the kids Sara hung out with were still reeling from the discovery of Diane Wallace's body and her funeral, they all felt relieved that the man who'd done it was behind bars. But their hopeful mood didn't last long.

Wednesday night the late news reported that another girl's body had been found. Mary Jo Rice, the senior who disappeared the previous spring, was found dead in a landfill outside of town. Efforts over the summer to relocate the landfill had finally won approval and men with bulldozers were working to move some of the overflow trash that accumulated in the original site. Late Wednesday afternoon they uncovered the girl's remains. It looked like her body had been hidden in the landfill not long after she'd been reported missing.

"Do you think that Lee Dumling guy told them where to look for Mary Jo?" Julie asked at lunch on Thursday.

Sara shook her head. "It said on the news that the workmen just stumbled on her body when they were moving stuff from the dump. I'll bet that if they hadn't decided to move the dump, they wouldn't have found her in a million years." She looked at LuAnn, who was glumly picking at her food. "What do you think?"

LuAnn just shrugged. "I don't know what's going on," she admitted finally. "But whatever it is, it's plenty strange. My dad has hardly been home except to sleep and he doesn't say anything to any of us."

That afternoon Sara arrived home to find Aunt Liz packed and ready to leave for Cincinnati. "Hi, honey. I've got to run. Ron—you remember him, my carpenter?—is picking me up any minute and driving me to the airport."

Sara interrupted with, "If I had a driver's license, I could take you there in your car."

Aunt Liz laughed understandingly. "We've got a month before your birthday. I'll try to think of some way to help you out by then. Now, there's tons of food in the freezer, so I know you won't starve. And here's Beth's number in case you need me. But I'm sure you won't—you're really very self-sufficient, Sara. I wish I'd had as much good sense at your age as you do."

Aunt Liz seemed to be rattling on a lot and

Sara wondered if she was nervous about leaving her in charge of the house. "I'll take care of everything. Don't worry," she reassured her aunt.

"Well, I must say I feel a whole lot better about leaving now that they've caught that guy. At least I won't have to lie awake nights wondering if you've been grabbed by some sicko."

"Oh, Aunt Liz," Sara wailed as she threw her arms around the older woman and gave her a hug. "I hope you haven't been doing that all along. I'm fine. Really."

Aunt Liz looked like she was about to cry, but she took a deep breath and smiled at Sara. "I know you are, honey. But you call me if you're concerned about anything. Anything at all. And if you decide to go out with your friends for dinner, just let Ted know. He's not as helpless in the kitchen as he likes to pretend. And he can always go to a restaurant." She took another breath and wrapped her arms around her niece. A pickup truck pulled into the driveway and honked. Aunt Liz hoisted her hanging garment bag to her shoulder and opened the front door. "Bye, honey. Take care of yourself. I'll see you on Sunday."

"Bye, Aunt Liz," Sara called to the departing figure. "Good luck with the job!"

As her aunt and Ron drove away, Sara shut the front door and suddenly the house seemed empty and alien. The bank of clouds that had hovered threateningly on the horizon all day began to move and soon cut off the late-afternoon sun. She shivered and found herself looking around a bit apprehensively. This is silly, she told herself. Aunt Liz is gone a lot; why are you acting like such a ninny? But she couldn't shake off the feeling of loneliness and fear, even after she was upstairs in her room studying.

Her mind refused to focus on the math book in front of her and eventually Sara gave up and called Julie. "I think my synapses have snapped or something," she explained. "Anyway, I'm calling it quits for now and thought I might be able to talk you into dinner at the mall."

"Oh, I don't know," Julie said dubiously. "I'm sitting here looking at a gigantic pile of laundry that my mom thought I might want to do while she and Dad are out at the theater. And then there's all this fascinating reading I've got to do before I start on my history term paper. You really think you can persuade me to give up the totally wonderful evening I have planned here at home?"

"It was just an idea," Sara said, pretending to be disappointed.

"I'll pick you up in five minutes!" Julie yelled into the phone.

As Sara climbed into Julie's mom's car Julie told her, "You're a lifesaver. I was about to go absolutely crazy. But how come you're not chained to the stove cooking for good old Uncle Ted?"

Sara laughed. "As a matter of fact, just before Aunt Liz left, she said something about how I might want to go out with my friends and not to worry about Uncle Ted's meals. So I figure she was giving me a hint. Anyway, he's a grown man. He can take care of himself."

"Whoa," Julie said. "I hope you don't say stuff like that to his face. He doesn't strike me as someone who responds well to smartmouth women."

Later, at the mall, they ran into Marsha and her mom shopping for dresses to wear to a cousin's upcoming wedding. Marsha's mom disappeared into a dressing room with an armload of clothes. "She'll be in there for hours," Marsha confided to the other two girls. "She tries everything on at least five times." She called to her mom through the dressing-room door, "I'm just going over to the food court with Julie and Sara. Come and find me when you're ready."

"So, did you hear the latest about that Lee Dumling guy?" Marsha asked once they were seated with an assortment of drinks and food in front of them.

"What now?" Julie asked. "Did he lead them to another body?"

Marsha shook her head. "No, that's the thing," she said around a mouthful of burrito. "It turns out that he probably didn't kill anybody."

"You're kidding!" Julie and Sara said in unison.

"Nope. My mom and I heard it on the news on the way over. He's got an alibi."

"How can he have an alibi? If he had someone who'd vouch for him, why wouldn't he say so right away when he was arrested?" Sara asked.

Marsha took another bite of her burrito and then said, "You aren't going to believe this, but it turns out that he was raping another girl in Trenton the same night Diane disappeared. That's why he didn't say anything sooner. But I guess his attorney got him to see that he was better off confessing to a rape than being stuck with a murder charge."

"Did he admit raping Marlene?" Julie wanted to know.

"Oh, yeah," Marsha said with a definite nod. "And both Marlene and the girl from Trenton positively identified him. He's going to be put away for a long, long time."

"But what about Diane and Mary Jo?" Sara asked in a frightened voice. "If he didn't kill them, then who did?"

Marsha's mom was waving frantically for her daughter to get going. "That's the big question now, isn't it?" Marsha said as she pushed back her chair and left.

The lights were on and Uncle Ted's car was in the driveway when Julie dropped Sara off that night. He called to Sara from the kitchen, where he was pouring himself a drink. "Did you girls have fun tonight?" His voice was friendly, and as he came into the living room he gave Sara a big smile.

"Uh, mostly we were studying together," Sara lied. "And I've still got a pile of work to do, so I'll go on up." She edged toward the stairs behind her, watching her uncle move closer.

"If you were studying so hard, where are your books?" he asked, still smiling.

Sara felt the first step of the staircase right behind her. "We were using Julie's books—she and I have a bunch of the same classes," she stammered. "I've really got to go. I'll see you in the morning." And she turned and ran up the stairs to her room.

Sara slammed the door behind her and turned the key in the lock. Her heart was pounding. What's the matter with you? she asked herself. She couldn't come up with a logical answer, but for some reason she'd started to feel kind of creepy around Uncle Ted. Get it together, she thought. He's only trying to be friendly. But Sara knew that the next two days while Aunt Liz was gone were going to be long ones for her.

Overton had a home game on Saturday afternoon and often Mike didn't take Sara out the night before the game, so she was especially pleased the next day at school when he suggested an early movie that night. "Sounds great," she told him. "But why don't you pick me up at Julie's? I've got to go over there after school anyway."

Later she asked Julie if it would be all right to meet Mike at her house. "Uncle Ted's going to have a fit if he knows that I'm seeing Mike two nights in a row. If he thinks I'm with you tonight, then tomorrow night won't be such a big deal."

"Sure, no problem," Julie said. "I'm going to the library after school to work on my term paper. Why don't you come with me and then we'll go to my house?"

After the movie Mike suggested pizza at Jake's. "Unless you're sick of it," he said with a laugh. "It must seem like there's no other place to go in Overton. I mean, even though this isn't L.A., we do have other restaurants."

"No, Jake's is fine," Sara assured him. "Actually it's nice to have one place where pretty much everyone hangs out. L.A. is so spread out that the chances of running into friends somewhere if you haven't already planned it are nil. Besides, I think I'm developing an addiction to Jake's special combo."

"Wait till I tell Jake. It'll make his day."

"You mean there really is a Jake?" Sara asked.

Mike laughed. "Of course there is. He's that little short guy with a limp who's always kind of hanging out there. He started the place when my dad was in school here and he knows more about what's going on in Overton than you can believe. I think he likes hanging around with the high-school kids—especially the girls! So be warned. I'm told he's tried to put the make on a few of them."

Sara laughed too. "I'll be careful," she promised.

After they ordered their pizza, Sara and Mike slid into the booth at the back that they liked to think of as "theirs." Mike held her hand across the table. "You know, you're really special, Sara," he said, looking into her eyes. "You're pretty and smart and a lot of fun to do stuff with. And you're not at all stuck on L.A. the way some people thought you might be."

"Some people being Rick," Sara said hotly. "And he still thinks that way."

Mike shrugged. "Rick's got his own problems."

"That's totally apparent. The question is how serious those problems are."

Mike gave Sara's hand a squeeze. "Hey, look, I'm trying to be romantic. I don't want to talk about Rick."

She grinned at him and squeezed his hand back. But just then the pizza and soft drinks arrived. "I give up," Mike said with a laugh, and grabbed a slice from the steaming pie.

A little while later Sara asked, "Did you hear about the rapist, that he isn't the one who killed Diane or Mary Jo?"

"Yeah, I think everybody did. And now the whole town is all terrorized again. For what? Two random murders in a year. I mean, I feel as terrible as anyone else about what happened to those two girls. But it doesn't mean we have a serial killer on the loose."

"The police think the same person killed them both," Sara pointed out.

Mike shrugged. "Well, the police might be wrong. Look, they thought that Lee Dumling killed Diane for a while, too, didn't they? I think it's just an act of chance. It's terrible, but those girls were simply in the wrong place at the wrong time."

Sara looked at him steadily. "Well, we know for sure when Diane disappeared, and it wasn't all that long ago. It was the night of the school elections. That's the night she was killed."

Suddenly Mike stared at her in horror. "Is that why you're so eager to find out where Rick was that night? You think he could have done that?"

"Well, it's a possibility. You said yourself that he has problems."

"Yeah, but that doesn't make him a murderer. Come on, Sara, that's crazy. You can't mean it— you can't possibly think this way."

"Look," Sara said, trying to sound reasonable, "you tell me what he was doing that night—a really good alibi—and I'll drop it. Until then, Rick is at the top of my list."

Mike gave Sara a serious look. "I think that California sun has baked your brain," he said, but then he saw the hot spots of anger forming on her cheeks. He rubbed his jaw and grumbled, "Okay, okay. I'll do it. I don't know how exactly, but I'll find out where he was, because I'm telling you, Rick couldn't have done it."

Luckily Uncle Ted was still out when Mike dropped Sara off that night. Thankful that she wouldn't have to explain why it was Mike who brought her home, she raced up to her room and speedily changed into her nightshirt. She wanted to be in bed and asleep by the time he came in. Sara didn't know what, if anything, had triggered the uneasiness she was feeling around her uncle. Maybe it was just an accumulation of little things that bothered her. Whatever it was, she knew that she'd have to work on overcoming it. She would be spending the rest of the school year here.

But she didn't have to overcome it tonight. Besides, she thought, the combination of a murderer on the loose and Aunt Liz being away was enough to make anyone jumpy. Maybe she'd feel differently once the murderer was caught.

CHAPTER 17

Sara hung out in her room doing homework Saturday morning until her uncle called up the stairs to her that he was heading out for the afternoon. One good thing about her aversion to him, she thought as she yelled down to remind him that she'd be going to the game and then out with Mike, was that she was getting a lot of studying done.

She was making herself a peanut-butter-and-jelly sandwich when the phone rang. It was Aunt Liz calling from Cincinnati. "How's everything going?" her aunt asked. After Sara assured her that all was well, Aunt Liz went on, "Well, you're not going to believe this—or maybe you are—but they want me to come in on Monday and meet the big boss, who's flying back to town to look over the finalists."

"Way to go!" Sara shouted into the phone. "I knew you could do it. You'll get that job for sure,

Aunt Liz. I have faith in you."

"I know you do, honey. And believe me, I'm doing my best to live up to your expectations," Aunt Liz said with a laugh. "Now, no one's exactly sure when this boss guy is showing up on Monday, and it may turn out that we'll all go out for dinner Monday night, so just to be on the safe side, I'll plan to stay over and fly home on Tuesday."

Sara's heart sank. As pleased as she was for her aunt, she hadn't considered that a Monday meeting would mean no Aunt Liz at home for another three days. "Okay," she said a little slowly.

Her aunt picked up on her tone of voice immediately. "What's the matter, Sara? You sound upset."

Sara made an effort to perk up. "Nothing's wrong. I'm getting ready to go to the game and then I'll be with Mike afterward. And everything is going fine. Maybe I just miss you."

Sara heard a catch in her aunt's voice as she said, "I miss you, too, Sara. I'm already lonely for you, thinking about your going home to L.A. after this year." She laughed at herself. "Listen to me—a couple of nights away and I'm sounding like some pathetic old lady. I'll see you before long. Take care, honey. I love you."

After she'd hung up, Sara wrote a note to Uncle Ted telling him about her aunt's change of plans. She stuck it under a magnet on the refrigerator and then went upstairs to dress for the game.

Sara couldn't help noticing that Melodie stayed as far away from her as was possible and still be on the same side of the field. Someone must have said something to her about how rotten everyone thought her stunt at the last game was. For a while Sara kept glancing at the other girl to see what she was up to, but after a while it became apparent that Melodie had decided that her best move was to leave Sara alone.

The game between the Overton Bulldogs and the Redfield Wildcats was a close one. Overton eventually won, but only after two fights on the field and one of the other team's players being sent out for unnecessary roughness.

Mike was in high spirits; this win put them one step closer to the state finals. By the time they got to Jake's, the place was crowded with boisterous students. "Come on, Sara, let's order and find a place to sit," he said as he plowed into the mass of well-wishers calling congratulations to him for making the winning touchdown.

A bunch of the guys were just vacating a booth in the back and they held it open for Sara and Mike. Sara scooted in and Mike slid in beside her. "There are bound to be people who want to join us, and I'm not going to be caught sitting across the table from you when I can be this close," he said with a grin, and put his arm around her. "Now, look," he went on, leaning close so that only she could hear, "before we get caught up in anything else, I want to get this Rick business straightened out. It wasn't easy, but I checked out where he was the night of the election. It was his birthday and he and his folks were out to dinner at Oscar's."

Sara opened her mouth to say something, but Mike stopped her. "Don't start in about how he could have snuck out of the house after they got home because Rick had a flat tire that afternoon and he didn't get it changed until the next day. A couple of the guys were complaining that he almost made them late for school because of it." He put his hand on the back of her neck. "Now are you satisfied? There's no way Rick could have killed Diane that night," Mike said with finality.

Although Sara was stubborn, she wasn't stupid. Much as she hated to admit it, Mike was right.

Throughout the rest of the evening it was as if Mike was the football king and Sara his queen and they were holding court. Kids stopped by to talk about the game, sat down and ate, and then drifted on while another bunch repeated the process. Sara couldn't remember when she'd ever felt this popular, basking in the enjoyment of Mike's reflected glory.

Eventually the crowd thinned out and Mike looked at his watch. "Oh, boy, it's late," he said. "Let's get going. I'm already on your uncle's bad side, I don't want to make it any worse."

The parking lot was almost empty, but as they

walked toward Mike's car another car screamed off the road and screeched to a stop just in front of them. Two big guys wearing Redfield letter jackets got out. They didn't look very steady on their feet and Sara could smell the beer on their breath ten feet away. "Oh, looky here, it's the big bad football star of the Overton Bullcraps," the taller one said with a sneer. "You telling this little honeybunch about what a hero you are?"

"Get out of here!" Mike's voice was low and angry.

"Sure, we'll leave," the other one said in a deceptively reasonable tone. Then he lunged forward and made a grab for Sara's arm. "We're just gonna take this cutie pie with us and show her a good time."

Mike punched the guy who'd tried to grab Sara. She screamed as the other one came flying around the car to swing at Mike. In seconds the three of them were brawling on the gravel surface of the parking lot.

Sara ran to the door of Jake's and yanked it open. "Help!" she screamed. "Two guys from Redfield are fighting with Mike!"

The man she knew to be Jake came limping to the door. "Call the cops!" he yelled back over his shoulder to the guy making pizza. Then he grabbed up a baseball bat from under the counter and went outside with Sara.

By the time they got there, Mike had already knocked one of the Redfield guys unconscious and was pummeling the other who was down on the ground. "That's enough!" Jake yelled. "He's done fighting."

Sara screamed at Mike to stop, but he just kept hitting the other guy. Finally, between the two of them, Jake and Sara managed to pull Mike away. Both of the Redfield guys lay in battered heaps on the gravel. Mike's face was a mess, but they both looked a lot worse.

"You better get out of here," Jake told Mike. "You got to take your girlfriend home and the cops are on their way. These guys ain't going nowhere. So go on, get out."

Mike stood there panting for a moment. Jake pulled a handkerchief from his pocket and handed it to him. As Mike dabbed at a cut on his cheek he said, "You're right, Jake. And thanks. I'm sorry to be leaving this trash in your parking lot." With a last spurt of anger he kicked at one of the Redfield guys, who looked like he was thinking of getting up.

They heard the wail of approaching sirens and Mike took Sara by the hand. "Come on. Jake can handle it from here on."

"Are you okay to drive?" Sara asked him as she gently touched an already forming bruise on his face.

Mike shrugged his shoulders and grinned. "You bet."

When they reached Sara's house, she wanted Mike to come inside so she could clean up his cuts. "Thanks, but I think I'd better just get on home," he told her at the front door. He was kissing her gently when the door abruptly swung open and Uncle Ted was standing there glaring at them.

"Do you know what time it is, young man?" Uncle Ted demanded. "I was worried sick. . . ." His voice trailed off as he took a good look at Mike's face. Immediately his eyes searched Sara for signs of injury. Relieved that she apparently wasn't hurt and suspicious of what had happened, he asked, "Were you in an accident?"

Mike and Sara both shook their heads. "Just a little disagreement," Mike told him.

"The other guys started it, Uncle Ted," Sara said quickly. "It wasn't Mike's fault. He was protecting me."

"Right," Uncle Ted said. He kept his tone as expressionless as possible. "Come inside, Sara. Say good night to your friend."

"But, Uncle Ted," Sara began.

"I better go. I'll talk to you tomorrow," Mike said to Sara. Then he faced her uncle. "I'm sorry we're late. It won't happen again."

Sara stood there watching Mike walk to his car while her uncle stood behind her. Finally she turned and went inside. Before she could utter a word, Uncle Ted said, "He's right. It won't happen again. Because you're not going out with him again."

"How can you say that?" Sara was appalled.

She'd never had anyone tell her what she could and couldn't do like that before.

Uncle Ted's mouth was a grim line. "Don't argue with me, Sara. You are not to see that fellow outside of school again. I want your word on that. If you disobey me, you'll find yourself grounded—permanently."

Tears of anger and humiliation ran down Sara's cheeks. "I can't believe I'm hearing this. You're a monster!" she yelled at him, and then ran upstairs to her room.

Once in her room, Sara found herself pacing the floor, trying to burn off all her pent-up anger. He can't do this, can he? she kept asking herself over and over. She knew her aunt would listen to reason, but it was way too late to call tonight. Tomorrow, Sara promised herself. Tomorrow I'll talk it over with Aunt Liz and she'll make everything right.

There was a tap at her door. "Who is it?" Sara asked heatedly even though there was only one person it could be.

Uncle Ted's voice was soft and sympathetic. "I'm sorry if you think I'm being overly harsh, Sara. Could you come out so we can talk about it?"

"No way," Sara yelled through the door. "I don't ever want to talk to you again."

She heard Uncle Ted sigh. "Very well. We'll let it go until tomorrow. Good night, Sara." She listened for his footsteps to recede down the hall and then flopped on her bed. Bunching her pillow against her, Sara sobbed until she fell asleep.

When the dream started this time, Sara was on the carousel and the man in the ski mask was chasing her. But suddenly Sara's huge carousel horse came to life and, leaping off the platform, raced through the crowded carnival. She looked over her shoulder. The man on his carousel horse was behind her and the gap between them was closing. Only now he no longer wore a ski mask.

Sara kept glancing back. She could see him so clearly except for his face. It remained shrouded in a mist that concealed his identity.

Sara's horse soared over the top of a fortune-teller's tent, and in the distance ahead Sara caught sight of another rider. She was a woman with flowing golden hair and a billowing crimson cloak atop a gleaming white horse, just like the fairy princess in a book Sara had loved as a child.

Suddenly Sara realized that the man wasn't chasing her after all. He was trying to catch the golden fairy princess. They were in a race, the man and Sara, to see who could get to the princess first. If Sara won, the princess would be saved; if the man reached the princess first, she was doomed.

Clinging to her horse's mane, Sara urged the animal to go faster. Her breath was coming in short gasps as the wind tore at her face and hair. A quick look back told her that the man was catching up. Soon he would pass her. I have to get to the princess before he does, Sara thought desperately.

Out of the corner of her eye, she saw the man pull alongside her. She turned her head and stared at him, but she still couldn't make out his face. Her mind screamed at her, Find out who he is. If you know who he is, you can save the princess!

Sara veered her horse toward the man. Maybe if she was closer, she could see his face. He knew what she was doing and he laughed at her. Then he kicked his horse's sides and the animal surged forward, leaving Sara behind. "No! No!" she screamed after him.

Sara awoke with a start, her heart pounding in fear. She was going to be too late to save the princess.

Her eyes adjusted to the darkness and Sara could see that she was safe inside her room. Still filled with the fear she'd had in the dream, she got up and walked to the window. Outside the night was calm and quiet. As she stood there her breathing eventually subsided to normal and slowly the dream faded from her mind.

You probably ate too much pizza, she told herself as she returned to bed and rearranged her comforter. But the thought that the dream was trying to tell her something important kept niggling at the back of her brain as she finally drifted off to sleep.

Sara awoke late on Sunday morning, and the minute she did, the whole ugly episode with Uncle Ted came flooding back. The thought of a discussion with him revolted her. Besides, it was sure to become a confrontation, one that she wasn't sure she could win by herself. I can't face him alone, she decided. I'll just stay away from him until Aunt Liz gets home.

But sticking with her determination to stay in her room all day if necessary became harder and harder. When the odor of frying bacon came wafting up the stairs, Sara realized that she was really hungry. She opened her door a crack and listened for sounds of movement downstairs. Maybe she could go on down and pretend he wasn't there. I just won't speak to him at all, she thought. Then she shook her head. Totally ignoring another person in the same house was simply beyond her.

Sara had just stepped back from the door when she was startled by Uncle Ted's voice booming up the stairs. "I'm going out for a while, Sara," he called. "We'll talk when I get back."

Overjoyed, Sara listened at her partially opened door until she heard his car pull out of the driveway. Then she raced down the stairs and into the kitchen. Grabbing a couple of strips of bacon from the plate next to the stove, she picked up the phone and dialed Julie's number.

CHAPTER 18

"Wait a minute! Slow down!" Julie demanded as Sara launched into a confused description of the argument she'd had with Uncle Ted the night before.

"He can't do this! It wasn't Mike's fault! Who does he think he is, anyway?" Sara rushed on.

Julie tried to make sense of the flood of words, but the only clear picture she had was that Sara was very upset and it had something to do with her uncle Ted and Mike. "Look," she said finally. "I can't use the car today, but I can get my mom to give me a ride over to your house in about an hour. How's that?"

"But what if he comes back?" Sara wailed.

Assuming that Sara was referring to her uncle, Julie said calmly, "Then we'll deal with him together."

By the time Julie's mom dropped her off, Sara had unsuccessfully tried to call Mike several times. At first the line had been busy and then the machine came on. On her third attempt Mike's mom answered the phone. She told Sara that Mike and his dad had gone to Youngstown to pick up Mike's grandmother and take her for a long drive in the country. They would probably stop somewhere to eat, and by the time they dropped the elderly woman off at her nursing home and drove back to Overton, it would be at least six o'clock.

"Would you tell Mike I called and that I'll call him back this evening?" Sara asked, trying to hide her disappointment.

"Do you want him to call you?" Mike's mom wanted to know.

Sara told her no, thanks, and hung up. She couldn't take the chance that Uncle Ted would pick up the phone when Mike called. That's all she'd need.

Julie took one look at Sara's anxiety-ridden face and said, "No wonder you're sounding nuts. You've been cooped up in the house when there's a beautiful day outside to enjoy. Besides, I think you need some exercise—it's supposed to be calming."

They'd walked about a mile before Sara had marshaled her thoughts enough to tell Julie the story clearly from beginning to end.

"So you ended up screaming at your uncle and then ran up and locked yourself in your room," Julie concluded when Sara had finished her tale.

"What was I supposed to do?" Sara demanded

indignantly. "Thank him for not listening to my side, treating me like a child, and generally ruining my life?"

Julie started to laugh. "Oh, I don't know. I probably would have done the same thing. At least you didn't get physical. I mean, throwing things is really tantrum city." Sara grinned and Julie said, "See, there's a little humor in every situation."

"Oh, Julie," Sara said, now laughing out loud, "you're so funny that I think you could make people see humor in the plague. But, seriously, I've got a real problem."

"Oh, yeah," Julie agreed. "First of all, your uncle's had a hate-on for Mike since the moment he saw him. Who knows why. Who cares. The fact is that all it took was one little excuse for him to go over the edge and tell you not to see Mike again." Sara nodded in agreement and Julie went on, "Secondly, your aunt is unavailable to run interference for you."

"I could call her," Sara volunteered.

Julie shook her head. "No, you can't. She's in the middle of a heavy stress situation herself, trying to land this big job. And besides, she's all the way over in Cincinnati. She's not going to be able to work her magic wiles on your uncle over the phone. So then you'll both be upset. And if she loses out on the job, you'll end up thinking it was because you got her all distracted with your problems."

Sara had to agree with Julie's reasoning. In fact, she'd already decided not to bother Aunt Liz with this until she got home and had only suggested she call in case Julie thought it was a good idea. "So, what do I do?" Sara asked.

"It's *we*, my dear, it's what do *we* do," Julie corrected her. "Since your aunt isn't here to make your uncle listen to reason, and since you certainly aren't the person to bring him around to another point of view, I'll have to step in and do it myself."

Sara stared at her friend in amazement. "How are you planning to do that?"

"Oh, I haven't worked that part out yet," Julie said airily. "The first thing we need to do is figure out what kinds of things about Mike would make your uncle see him in a better light."

"Like?" Sara wanted to know.

"Like your uncle doesn't think much of the fact that Mike plays football. Thinks he's just a dumb jock, right?" Julie paused while Sara nodded. "Well, what if Uncle Ted found out that Mike had decided to become a hotshot attorney and had just gotten a full scholarship to Harvard because he not only plays football but is smart besides?"

"Are you nuts? Mike doesn't have a clue what he wants to do, and his dad is just hoping he'll get a football scholarship somewhere."

Julie grinned mischievously. "That's what you and I know, but that isn't what your uncle necessarily needs to know."

"But he'll find out," Sara protested.

Julie shrugged. "So by that time you tell him that Mike changed his mind or whatever you think of at the moment. The important thing is to get your uncle to start looking at Mike as someone he wants his precious niece to hang out with."

Sara shook her head dubiously. "I don't think I could tell Uncle Ted anything like what you're suggesting with a straight face."

"Oh, you're not telling him any of it. I am. The only thing you're going to say to him is that you're sorry. That you were wrong."

"What!" Sara was stunned at this betrayal.

"Look, you don't have to mean it. But the only way he'll listen to either of us is if you start things off by apologizing. That way he'll think he's got the upper hand. Then he'll let his guard down."

The two of them turned the corner and headed back toward Sara's, working out the details of their plan along the way.

By the time Uncle Ted got home, Julie and Sara had raided the freezer and concocted a truly elegant meal. The table was set with the good china and silver, and they'd even resorted to candles for effect.

The hardest part for Sara was apologizing to him. But she greeted him at the door by telling him how sorry she was to have behaved so badly. She found that she couldn't face him, but her downcast eyes must have added to the pathos of her extensive apology, and eventually Uncle Ted told her it was all over and forgotten.

In the kitchen, preparing a drink and a plate of hors d'oeuvres for him, Sara and Julie could barely suppress their giggles. "You'll get the lead in the school play for sure," Julie told Sara. "You're a natural."

Throughout the rest of the evening Sara was relieved to discover that she didn't have to add much to the conversation. Julie made a point of charming Uncle Ted. She listened wide-eyed to all of his stories and urged him to tell more. She laughed at all his dumb jokes and then told even dumber ones herself.

Finally Julie introduced Mike's name into the conversation. Later Sara still wasn't sure how she'd done it, but before long Julie was telling Uncle Ted how she wished she could have a boyfriend as smart and protective and all-around wonderful as Mike. Sara was amazed to see that her uncle was lapping it up, all the while assuring Julie that she was such a pretty girl that he couldn't believe she didn't have great boyfriends of her own. And Julie, girl of a thousand dates, just sat there pretending that she stayed home all the time because she couldn't find anyone as nice as Mike.

Finally dinner was over. Sara felt as if she'd been holding her breath through the entire meal, waiting for Uncle Ted to figure out what was going on. He'd even bought the Harvard scholarship story without batting an eye.

Sara was looking forward to spending some time alone with Julie while they cleaned up the kitchen. But to her astonishment Uncle Ted insisted on helping.

Finally Julie looked at her watch. "I think I'd better be getting home," she said. "I'll call my mom."

"Don't be silly," Uncle Ted told her. "I'll give you a ride." He smiled at Julie. "After that great dinner you served, it's the least I can do."

Sara handed Julie her jacket from the hall closet and was pulling out her own when Uncle Ted told her, "No, Sara, you better stay here. Liz might call."

"So she'll leave a message on the machine and we'll call her back when we get home," Sara said matter-of-factly. "Then we'll both get to talk to her."

"No!" Uncle Ted's tone didn't allow for argument. "I may have some errands to run after I drop Julie off and I'm sure you have homework to do," he added more reasonably.

Julie turned to Sara so her back was to Uncle Ted. "Yeah, I know you've got stuff you didn't get to today," she agreed. Then she mouthed, "Like call Mike," and winked at Sara.

Sara stood at the open door watching the two of them drive off. Something about their leaving bothered her but she couldn't put her finger on it. Sighing, she shut the door and went to the phone.

This time no one was home at Mike's and Sara hung up without leaving a message. Had his mother said something about them all going out to dinner after Mike and his dad got back from visiting his grandmother? She didn't remember, but she certainly didn't want him calling and talking to Uncle Ted tonight. What a disaster it would be if Uncle Ted started congratulating Mike on his scholarship!

Sara looked at the clock on the mantel. It would take Uncle Ted ten minutes tops to drive Julie home, so he might not be gone for long. Why hadn't she asked him about the errands he'd said something about doing? Then she'd be better able to gauge when he'd be back. While Uncle Ted had been totally charming all evening, Sara didn't feel up to chatting with him on her own. It wasn't so bad when Julie was there to keep the conversation going, just like Aunt Liz kept things humming along when she was home. For a fleeting instant Sara wondered if Aunt Liz was playacting all the time like Julie had been doing. Then the clock chimed.

Julie would be home by now. Sara decided to call and tell her what a spectacular job she'd done with Uncle Ted. I still think he's kind of a creep, she realized while she was dialing Julie's number. No matter how nice he was tonight, I don't really trust him.

"I thought you might be Julie calling for a ride," Julie's mom said when she answered the phone.

"You mean she's not home yet?" Sara asked. "Well, she should be there soon. Ask her to call me as soon as she gets in." Sara hung up and nervously paced around the living room, frequently glancing out the window for headlights in the driveway. She hoped Julie would call soon. It would be awful if her uncle walked in on her when she was giggling with Julie about how well their plan had worked.

Another ten minutes passed. Why hadn't Julie called? Her mother probably forgot to give her my message, Sara decided as she dialed the number again. But Julie still wasn't home, and now her mom was sounding worried. "Oh, they might have had a flat or something," Sara said, trying to reassure both of them. "Or maybe my uncle decided to take care of some of his errands on the way to your house."

Sara hung up the phone and stared at it for a long moment. There was something wrong and now she knew what it was. Uncle Ted hadn't looked like someone giving his niece's teenage girlfriend a ride home on the way to run errands. He'd acted like a man going out on a date. The way he'd helped Julie on with her jacket, the way he'd casually put his hand on her shoulder and opened the car door for her—that wasn't how Uncle Ted usually was.

Was it possible that Uncle Ted had misinter-
preted Julie's enthusiasm all evening? Could he
have thought she was coming on to him? Sara
sneered at the idea. The thought that anyone her
age would be interested in Uncle Ted was ridicu-
lous.

Wait a minute, she said to herself. If he did
think that, why would he encourage it? She and
Julie were only teenagers and her uncle was
old enough to be Julie's father and then some.
There'd have to be something really wrong with
a man that age making a play for a junior in
high school.

And what if he did come on to Julie? Sara
winced as this new thought crossed her mind.
She could see Julie laughing her head off if
some old guy like her uncle tried to kiss her or
something. In her mind's eye she saw the scene;
she could almost feel her uncle's flashing anger.
What would he do then? Rape her? Try to throttle
her when he realized she'd tell everyone what a
fool he'd been?

Sara's hands flew to her mouth. "Oh, no," she
cried aloud. Her dream and reality merged and
suddenly Sara felt certain that her uncle was a
killer.

Where would he take Julie? Sara's thoughts
swarmed over the possibilities and then she
remembered the conversation about the old
family barn out on Smithtown Road. What had
Uncle Ted said—that if he were going to kill a

girl, he'd take her out there? Why hadn't they really listened to him? It was almost as good as a confession and she and Aunt Liz had treated it like a joke. That's where he'd killed Diane Wallace and Mary Jo Rice.

Her fingers moving automatically, Sara dialed Mike's number. The machine was on, and as Sara listened to its recorded message she wondered if she had totally gone off the deep end. Not liking your uncle was one thing, but thinking he was a killer was another. What if there was an innocent explanation to the whole thing?

In her heart she knew she was right. What she should be doing was calling the cops. But she couldn't take the chance and accuse him without being sure. If she was wrong and she brought in the police, her life in Overton with Aunt Liz and Uncle Ted would be unbearable.

When her turn came to leave a message, Sara tried to think of something that would get Mike's attention without really saying what she feared. "Mike, it's Sara and it's almost nine-fifteen. Please, please meet me right away at my uncle's old deserted barn out on Smithtown Road. It's a matter of life and death." It was the best she could do.

Next Sara opened the drawer of the ornate hall stand where all the keys in the house seemed to end up. Sure enough, the keys to Aunt Liz's Explorer were there. She yanked on her jacket, made sure she had a house key, and went outside.

For a fleeting instant as she started her aunt's car, Sara wondered if Uncle Ted would be madder at her driving without a license than he would have been if she'd called the cops. Thankful that her aunt had a car with automatic transmission, Sara carefully backed out of the driveway.

She'd seen the old family barn from the highway in daylight several times. Once when she and Mike had taken a drive, she'd pointed it out to him. Now she hoped she could find it in the dark. It sat beyond a field in a grove of trees and a rutted lane led to it from the main road, but the deserted place would have no lights at night to guide her.

A couple of times Sara was sure she'd gone too far and passed it, but finally her headlights picked up the forlorn For Sale sign dangling by one hook from a post by the road. She turned onto the lane that led to the barn, keeping a close watch for Uncle Ted's car. One part of her prayed she was wrong and that by now Julie was safe at home; the other part feared she was right and that she would be too late to save her friend.

CHAPTER 19

As Sara neared the stand of trees surrounding the derelict barn a feeling of relief washed over her. Uncle Ted's car was nowhere to be seen. So I got a little crazy, she thought. At least no one knows what I actually was thinking. She decided she'd find a pay phone on the way back into town and call Mike. She'd tell him she'd had a stress attack and not to worry; if she got his machine, so much the better. Then she could cancel her previous message and figure out what to tell him tomorrow.

The lane was too narrow at this point to turn around. And the one thing she definitely didn't want to do was damage Aunt Liz's car. It would be bad enough if Uncle Ted beat her home and realized she'd been driving. Even a little scratch on the fender would be all he'd need to ban her from driving for the rest of the year.

She drove slowly toward the derelict barn, hoping to find a smooth open space to turn around in. The lane ran alongside the barn and around to the back, so Sara followed it. Sure enough, at the other side was a wide open spot. Sara swung the wheel, and as her headlights raked through the trees next to the cleared area, she jammed on her brakes. Uncle Ted's car was nestled among the trees and bushes at the edge of the clearing.

Immobilized, Sara clutched the steering wheel, her hands slippery with sweat. She felt as if she couldn't breathe, and her heart was pounding so hard she thought her chest would explode. It is Uncle Ted, she thought wildly. And Julie must be here with him. I've got to do something!

Finally Sara regained enough control to move her hands and feet. Shakily she completed the turn and drove the Explorer back around the side of the barn, stopping in the middle of the narrow lane leading out to the highway. She turned off the engine, opened the window, and listened. Fear emanated from her like a bad odor.

Quietly Sara opened the car door, slid out from under the wheel and then pushed the door almost closed. Then she crept back to the barn, and keeping to the trees for cover, she moved toward her uncle's car. At every step she expected him to jump out at her. How could he not have seen her arrive when her headlights shone right into his windshield?

A few moments later she knew the answer. When she reached the car, it was empty. They had to be in the barn.

There were big barn doors at the back, but Sara couldn't imagine opening one of them without the whole world knowing. By now her eyes were more accustomed to the dark and she saw the faint outline of a smaller door cut into one of the big ones. She ran across the clearing and grabbed the rope pull of the smaller door. Then she hesitated. All around her were the sounds of country—breeze rustling through the trees, the flapping of a night bird overhead. No voices, no human noises. Where were they? Was Julie still alive? Was Uncle Ted waiting beyond that door for her to walk in so he could kill her too?

Then Sara heard Julie scream, breaking the spell of fear. She yanked open the barn door and rushed inside. The roof of the barn was partially destroyed and moonlight filtered in through the gap, providing as much illumination as there was outside.

"Get your hands off me!" Julie yelled. Her voice was coming from the rafters above Sara's head, and soon she saw a ladder leading to the hayloft.

"Julie, baby, you know you want me," Uncle Ted crooned. "You told me so yourself."

"Get real! No one in her right mind would want you, you creep!" she screamed at him.

Sara could hear them scuffling in the straw as she climbed the ladder. Now that she was almost up there, she realized that she should have looked around for a weapon down below in the barn. Her uncle was a big and powerful man. Could she and Julie fight him off between them?

Julie let out a shriek, and when Sara poked her head above the hayloft floor, she saw that her uncle had Julie by the arm and was twisting it. "We can do this the easy way or the hard way," he growled.

"Let her go!" Sara yelled at him as she scrambled up the last steps of the ladder onto the hayloft.

Uncle Ted spun around while Julie screamed, "Help! Sara! Get him away from me, he's nuts!"

He grabbed Julie by the hair. "Don't come any closer, Sara. Just go home and we'll pretend you never saw this. It'll be our little secret."

With a scream of her own, Sara rushed at him and knocked both of them down. She pummeled her uncle's face and body until he let go of Julie to defend himself. Julie twisted out of reach and then jumped on him, landing on his chest with her knees. They heard the breath go out of him and for a moment he lay still. Then suddenly he roared out at them, flailing out to grab them as he struggled to his feet. One hand snagged Julie's hair again and the other caught Sara by the arm.

Both girls were kicking and screaming and beating at him as hard as they could, but none of it seemed to faze him. Like an automaton he dragged them to the edge of the hay loft. "Looks like you two girls are going to have a very nasty accident," he snarled.

Now, instead of trying to get away from him, they both clung to him hoping he wouldn't risk falling himself in his attempt to throw them over the edge.

"You did it, didn't you, Uncle Ted?" Sara gasped. "You killed those two girls from school."

Her uncle snorted in disgust. "Tramps, both of them. Just like you two. Lead a man on and then when he does what comes naturally, they cry and say they'll tell." He smiled grimly at Sara. "Now I couldn't let that happen, could I?"

Sara's thoughts raced. What could she say to disarm him? "We won't tell, Uncle Ted," Sara pleaded. "Please let us go and we'll be good. Won't we, Julie?"

But Julie was too angry to go along with the lie. "You filthy scum!" she yelled at him. "No girl in her right mind would lead you on—you're too disgusting!" She spat in his face.

With a howl of rage, Uncle Ted let go of Sara to take a swing at Julie. In that moment Sara moved around behind him and grabbed Julie's arm, yanking her out of her uncle's grasp. Then she shoved him toward the edge of the hayloft.

He teetered over the precipice and somehow managed to get hold of the ladder as he was

falling. The momentum and his weight clinging to the top of the ladder pulled the ladder
away from the lip of the hayloft. Julie and Sara
moved closer to the edge and watched. As if in
slow motion, the whole thing toppled over and
crashed to the floor of the barn. Uncle Ted lay
still beneath the fallen ladder.

The two girls stared down, clinging together
in shocked silence. Then, in the uncertain light
from the moon, they saw him move. Slowly he
pushed the heavy ladder away and slid out from
under it. He staggered to his feet and glared up
at them. "I'll get you! I'll get you both! I don't
know when, but I'll do it," he screamed. As he
moved toward the barn door they saw that his
left arm was dangling strangely.

Trembling, the girls watched him lurch
through the doorway. After a moment they
heard a car start up. Then headlights swept
across the space below them as the car turned
and gathered speed.

"He can't get past Aunt Liz's car," Sara whispered. Even as she spoke they heard the shriek
of metal against metal; he must have squeezed
past the Explorer in the narrow lane. They could
hear the engine roar as he accelerated and sped
toward the main road.

Shakily the two girls backed away from the
edge of the hayloft. Sara found she was clutching
Julie's hand as they stood there in the dusty old
hay that still covered the floor of the loft.

Suddenly, farther away, there was the sound of a car crashing into something.

Sara's thoughts were a jumble of confusion. She couldn't tell if the car had kept going on the main road or not. Had the monster—she couldn't think of him as Uncle Ted anymore—killed himself smashing into a tree? Or was he unhurt by the crash and even now stealthily making his way back to the barn?

Sara and Julie stared at each other, their eyes wide with fear. In unconscious unison they shrank back farther into the corner of the hayloft. They both knew there was no way for them to escape. They were trapped.

CHAPTER 20

Rapid footsteps thudded on the hard-packed dirt of the lane. He was coming back! Sara's heart seemed to stop beating and she gazed for a moment in frozen terror toward the open door of the barn. Then, tearing her eyes away, she peered wildly around the hayloft, hoping to spot in one of its dim corners something to use as a weapon.

"Sara!" Someone burst through the doorway and shouted again. "Sara! Where are you? Are you okay?"

It was Mike! Gasping in relief, Sara ran forward. "I'm up here. Oh, Mike, we've got to get down—he might come back! He tried to kill us!" As he stared up in confusion she pointed at the barn floor. "The ladder!"

He bent down and, with a grunt of effort, raised the far end of the heavy wooden ladder. Describing a slow arc in the air, it fell with a crash against the edge of the hayloft. Quickly checking to make sure it was steady, Mike scrambled up to where the girls stood.

"Oh, Sara!" His strong arms went around her, crushing her close to him.

Sara sagged against him in relief. Then she heard Julie's urgent voice. "Come on, we've got to get out of here!"

It was nearly impossible for Sara to turn her back to the door—she felt so exposed as she put her foot on the top rung of the ladder. But Mike's steadying presence gave her courage, and somehow they all slithered down to the barn's floor.

Julie was already at the door. "Come on!" she urged again.

Clutching Mike's hand, Sara pulled him toward the shadowy opening. "She's right, he could be coming back!"

Mike shook his head. "If you mean your uncle Ted, he's long gone. He smashed into me at the entrance to the lane and took off down the road. Besides, the cops should be here any minute."

"The cops?" Julie and Sara stared at him in amazement, and then Sara could hear sirens in the distance.

"Sure, you don't think I'd come out here without calling them first, do you?" He stopped for a moment and then said, "I don't know what's been going on, but when I got your message, I knew something must be really wrong. But I didn't want us all to be embarrassed if it turned out to be a mistake. So I called LuAnn's dad—he's been pretty decent to me when I've gotten into a couple of scrapes. I figured he'd meet me here, and if it was nothing, then no one else would need to know." He stared at Sara and then at Julie. "But what did happen? And what are you doing here, Julie?"

They both began to explain what had gone on since Julie had left Sara's house with Uncle Ted, but the jumbled tale didn't make much sense because they kept backtracking and interrupting each other. And before they could make everything clear, they were momentarily blinded by brilliant searchlights as a police cruiser bucketed toward them along the lane. LuAnn's father leaped out and strode across to the three teenagers.

"Julie? Is that you? Are you okay?" As she nodded he turned to Sara. "And you're Sara Langdon?"

"Yes." Her voice was shaky.

Looking back toward his car, Sergeant Philips yelled, "Hey, Don, call in and tell them both girls are here and they seem okay." Then he said to Julie, "Your mom's been calling us—she's worried sick about you." Including them both, he asked, "What's going on?"

By now Sara and Julie were able to tell their story more or less coherently. Sergeant Philips interrupted a couple of times to give instructions to his partner, and before long the barn was filled with activity.

Both Sara and Julie were trembling from exhaustion by the time they'd finished. LuAnn's dad looked at them sympathetically. "You girls look done in," he said kindly. "Must have been pretty terrifying for you both. I'll have someone drive you home. You can come down to the station tomorrow and make a full statement."

Another policeman came up to them and drew Sergeant Philips away, muttering something that Sara couldn't catch. As the policeman left again LuAnn's dad walked over to Sara and put his arm around her shoulders. "Sara, I'm afraid there's more bad news. Your uncle's car went out of control out toward Trenton and—well, he was dead by the time the troopers got to him."

For the first time since the whole nightmare had begun, Sara began to cry. "Oh, poor Aunt Liz! And she doesn't even—she's out of town and the number where she's staying is at home," she sobbed. "I've got to call her."

"There's no one else at the house?" LuAnn's dad asked. When Sara shook her head, he went on, "Well, you're not staying there alone. Can she sleep over with you tonight, Julie?"

"Of course," Julie told him while she put her arms around her friend.

"Then we'll pick up the number on the way to Julie's and you can call your aunt from her house." LuAnn's dad's tone was decisive.

Dazed, Sara nodded mutely. She swayed slightly on her feet and then Mike's arm was around her. Gratefully she leaned back and let the warmth of his concern support her.

Sergeant Philips was saying, "We'll get the tow truck to take your car in to Barney's Service— that's where you want it?" Mike nodded and he went on, "Okay, then I'll get Don to drive all of you home." He turned to Sara once more. "Tell your aunt—well, I'm just sorry all this had to happen." Shaking his head, he walked toward the group of police officers by the barn door.

Mike walked the girls out to Aunt Liz's Explorer and held Sara close for a long moment before she climbed into the backseat with Julie. Then he got in the front with the policeman.

Once at Sara's house, they all trooped inside— Sara and Julie, the policeman who'd driven them, and Mike. Sara found the note Aunt Liz had left and with shaking hands dialed the number in Cincinnati.

By the time Sara neared the end of the conversation with her aunt, she was crying so hard she could barely speak. Julie took the receiver out of her hand. When she hung up a few minutes later, she told them, "Sara's aunt is going to take the early flight tomorrow morning—there's nothing going out tonight. I told her my mom would pick her up."

At last Sara and Julie were alone in Julie's room with the door closed behind them. The emotional intensity of saying good night to Mike

and greeting Julie's overwrought parents had
left both girls exhausted. But they were still
too keyed up to sleep. They sat on Julie's bed,
propped up with pillows and enveloped in a
fluffy comforter. After several long moments
Sara finally asked, "Julie, what happened?"

"Well, I've got to admit it took me a long time
to figure out that he was coming on to me," Julie
admitted slowly. "I mean, I never imagined that
your uncle would think—" She caught her breath
and Sara shuddered.

After a moment Julie went on. "Anyway, he
said it was such a nice night that we ought to
take a little drive and enjoy it. He wanted to take
me out to this old farm his family had owned
forever. He told me it was incredibly beautiful
at night with the moon and stars and all." She
gulped before continuing. "I figured that it would
give me more of a chance to sing Mike's praises,
so I said okay. Then, when we got there, he
parked in the trees and wanted to get out and
take a walk."

Sara's hands clenched themselves into tight
fists as Julie's voice went on quietly. "I should
have known then that something was wrong.
And I did think he was acting more interested
in me than he was in my stories about you and
Mike. But when he put his arm around me
while we were walking, I couldn't believe it.
And then he tried to kiss me."

Even though she'd known it was coming, Sara felt her body turn cold with disgust. "What did you do?" she whispered.

Julie gave a shaky little laugh. "Well, you know me—never at a loss for words. I just kept talking."

"All that time?" Sara asked, staring at her friend incredulously.

"Oh, yeah. By then it didn't take a brain surgeon to realize what he wanted. So I thought, if I can keep him talking then maybe I'll eventually figure some way out of this. I asked him about the farm and about his family and how it was when he was growing up. I even got him talking about the kinds of animals they used to have on that farm when he was a kid. Believe me, Sara, I came up with every dumb topic I could think of."

"But then what? How did you end up in the hayloft?" Sara didn't really want to hear the details, but on another level she felt she had to know in order to keep the horrors in her own mind at bay.

"Oh, that," Julie said, shaking her head at her own stupidity. "Finally I started running out of things to say, so I told him that I'd like to look inside the barn. When I saw the ladder, I asked him where it went. I mean, what do I know about barns? So he suggested we go on up and take a look. I kept thinking I'd find a way to run off and leave him stranded. He'd left his keys in the car, and if I could get away from him long enough, I was sure I could take his car and drive off."

Sara put her arms around Julie. "But it didn't work out that way, did it?"

Julie shook her head, tears streaming down her face. "I was trapped up there. With him. He kept talking about other girls, how they'd pretended to be interested in him, but he could tell that I really cared. He told me that he'd wanted me since the first time he saw me at your house, that I was his dream girl." She gulped and for a moment she was reliving the scene in her mind. Then she said, "I really considered just letting him do it, you know? I thought I could lie there with my eyes closed and pretend he was someone else. I hoped after it was over that he'd take me home, or at least take me out of there so I could get away."

Julie looked at Sara, her eyes full of anguish. "But I just couldn't do it, Sara. I couldn't make myself. I don't know what would have happened if you hadn't showed up."

I'm afraid I do, Sara thought. Her own eyes brimmed with tears. Julie could have ended up the way Diane and that other girl, Mary Jo, did. The whole thing still didn't seem real to Sara, but underneath she knew it was true.

For a long time the two friends sat nestled together on the bed, each lost in her own thoughts. But at last they dropped into uneasy sleep.

CHAPTER 21

The week that followed was the longest Sara had ever lived through. On Sunday evening she and Aunt Liz were sitting in the living room after supper. A cold snap had swept through the region and Sara cupped her hands around her mug of steaming hot chocolate. The flames dancing in the fireplace seemed to create an oasis of comforting safety.

Tucking her feet under her, Sara gazed into the flickering light and thought about everything that had happened since last Sunday night. She felt as if she'd gone through it all like a robot, doing and saying whatever was necessary but not taking it in. But now she might be ready to sort it out and try to make sense of the tragedy that had overtaken them.

Almost the worst had been meeting Aunt Liz at the airport. Her face had been haggard and drawn with shock and Sara had been afraid that her aunt might collapse at any moment. But she hadn't, and her main concern seemed to be about Sara. She'd kept saying how guilty she felt about letting Sara be touched by this horror. "If only I'd known!" she'd said over and over, though Sara tried to assure her aunt that it wasn't her fault.

Sara could barely remember the long interviews with the police. The officers she'd talked to had all been kind and very patient, but she hoped she'd never have to go through such an ordeal again. She had gathered, though, that they'd found some sort of evidence linking Uncle Ted to the deaths of both Diane Wallace and Mary Jo Rice. Their families must feel relieved at least to know for sure what had happened.

Aunt Liz of course had called Sara's dad in South America, and when he'd returned the call, Sara and her aunt had had to tell him the whole terrible story. He'd said he would come up to be with them right away, but Sara had finally convinced him to wait until the critical phase of his research was over in a couple of weeks. It was odd—she'd thought at the beginning that she wanted him there for her to lean on, but then she'd realized that she first needed to work things through with the people who'd been involved.

And then there had been the funeral. Sara had dreaded it, but it hadn't been nearly as bad as she'd feared—only a small private ceremony at the grave side. The ritual had been unexpectedly comforting, and even Aunt Liz had looked a little less strained and tense when it was over.

Aunt Liz had hardly cried at all during the first few days. But the day after the funeral, Mr. Palmer, the minister who conducted the service, had come to see them. He'd spent a long time talking with Aunt Liz, and it seemed to Sara that somehow he'd given her aunt permission to weep. Even more important, after his visit, Aunt Liz didn't seem to be blaming herself so much for her husband's crimes.

Sara herself had cried a lot all week long—she felt as if there wasn't a single tear left. It would be a long time—maybe never—before she would understand how anyone could do the terrible things Uncle Ted had done. And though it didn't make sense, the whole thing had left her feeling dirty and ashamed.

In fact, the only good part of the entire week had been the reaction of Sara's friends. Naturally she'd spent a lot of time with Julie and with Mike—the traumatic experiences they'd shared had drawn them even closer to one another. But she was unprepared for the sympathy and concern the kids from school had poured out. Sara hadn't realized until now how many friends she'd made in Overton.

She glanced at the other end of the couch and found Aunt Liz gazing at her with a troubled expression. Meeting Sara's eyes, Aunt Liz said quietly, "Have you thought yet what you want to do about school?"

Sara had stayed home all week—she hadn't felt able to face large groups of people and she knew that concentrating on schoolwork was beyond her. But she couldn't stay away forever. "I guess I'll go back tomorrow," she answered slowly. "I'm probably as ready as I'm going to be."

Aunt Liz nodded. "That's good, Sara." Still gazing intently at her niece's features, so like her own, she took a deep breath. "But what I really meant was, how do you feel about staying in school here in Overton?"

Puzzled, Sara didn't reply. Her aunt's voice was husky as she explained, "I wondered if when your dad gets here, you'll want to go back home to California. I mean, I wouldn't blame you if you felt you wanted to leave Overton and all that's happened here and never come back again."

Sara stared at Aunt Liz. What was she trying to say? *Maybe taking care of me is going to be too much of a burden for her now.* Then a worse thought crept into her mind—*perhaps I'm a terrible reminder of the whole tragedy and she just wants me out of her sight.* Her eyes filled with tears. "Do you want me to leave, Aunt Liz?"

"Oh, Sara, no!" Aunt Liz's voice held such sincerity that Sara couldn't doubt it.

"Because I don't want to," she said through the lump in her throat.

Aunt Liz moved toward Sara and reached out to fold her in her arms. "Sara, honey, I'm so glad. I wish you could stay here forever."

Sara managed a shaky laugh. "I don't know about forever, Aunt Liz, but . . ."

As her words trailed off, the sentence completed itself in Sara's mind: but maybe I'll stay here until I'm out of high school. The idea took root and blossomed. Of course, she'd have to talk it over with Dad, but Sara was sure he would agree. And the more she thought about it, the surer she felt that it was what she wanted.

The phone rang, startling both of them. It was Mike. "Hi, Sara, how are you doing?" he asked. But before she could answer, he went on, "I was wondering if you felt like going for a ride or something."

"Oh, Mike, not tonight—Aunt Liz and I have a lot of stuff to talk over. But I'm going to school tomorrow."

"Great! I'll pick you up—around eight o'clock?"

Sara smiled. "Fine, I'll be ready."

Order Form

To order direct from the publishers, just make a list of the titles you want and fill in the form below:

Name ....

Address ....

....

....

Send to: Dept 6, HarperCollins Publishers Ltd, Westerhill Road, Bishopbriggs, Glasgow G64 2QT.

Please enclose a cheque or postal order to the value of the cover price, plus:

UK & BFPO: Add £1.00 for the first book, and 25p per copy for each addition book ordered.

Overseas and Eire: Add £2.95 service charge. Books will be sent by surface mail but quotes for airmail despatch will be given on request.

A 24-hour telephone ordering service is avail-able to Visa and Access card holders: 041-772 2281